Tammy,

Hope this Captures your attention
and inspires! Madison
Avery

CAPTURING
the MUSE

Madison Avery

NAKED PUBLISHING

Stark Naked Publishing

Hamilton, Ontario

Stark Naked Publishing
Hamilton, Ontario

Publisher's Note: This is a work of fiction. Names, characters, places, and incidents are a product of the author's imagination. Locales and public names are sometimes used for atmospheric purposes. Any resemblance to actual people, living or dead, or to businesses, companies, events, institutions, or locales is completely coincidental.

Book Layout © 2014 BookDesignTemplates.com

Capturing the Muse / Madison Avery – 1st print edition (2015)

eBook ISBN - 978-0-9948145-1-7
Print ISBN 978-0-9948145-0-0

Dedication

To the muse that left, and the new one I captured.

Contents

Authors Note

I'VE READ several books lately that have included an Authors Note. I kinda like the idea. This isn't where I thank everyone that helped me get this book together, you'll have to wait for that, or skip to the end. This is where I tell you a bit of the inspiration behind this book. This... collected work of short stories.

The thing about writing is this: it's not easy. It's not. It's impossibly hard. And I think every author I know, and even ones I don't, have probably thought a time or two about giving up. Or having hit a wall so high, and hard, carved out of stone, that they can't seem to break through it, or know how to scale it. There are no easy ways to combat this type of moment. Or rather, moments that seem to stretch the length of time; days turning into weeks, and months, and then, maybe even years.

We, in the industry, call this Writer's Block. It's sort of funny—it is—that writers are the only collective profession in the world that have given a word to some unforeseen force that takes over and allows them not to work. Not to get the job done.

"All writing is difficult. The most you can hope for is a day when it goes reasonably easily. Plumbers don't get plumber's block, and doctors don't get doctor's block; why should writers be the only profession that gives a special name to the difficulty of working, and then expects sympathy for it?"

~ *Philip Pullman*

I never used to believe in Writer's Block. I thought it was just an excuse, or something imaginary in the mind that writers gave too much power to, and eventually, it just takes over. I was the person with a million ideas, stories that begged to be written, that constant hum, or whisper, that I attributed to my Muse. My mythical friend that helped guide my way. I woke up and was desperate to let my fingers caress the keyboard and allow words to flow through me, creating works of brilliant and masterful art; or at least, what I thought was brilliant and masterful art, that part was (and always will be) up for debate.

But then, one day, it was gone. That whispering Muse, the inkling to write, that desperation to release my innermost thoughts and desires onto a page, for fear if I didn't, I'd explode. It was just gone. I lost that motivation. That courage. I had let the imaginary Writer's Block get the best of me. Days turned into weeks, eventually leading the way to months and before I knew it, almost a whole year had passed. Sure, I wrote things: Grocery Lists, and To-Do Lists, and maybe when I heard that barest hint of my Muse speaking to me, I'd write a little more, but it never amounted to much. I could never seem to harness the voice, control it, and force it to help me write something of substance.

I truly had begun to think it was gone. Forever. That I had written the creativity right out of me. But that seemed, and felt, just as absurd as admitting I was suffering from Writer's Block. I had given in, and given it too much power, and it began to consume me. And deep down, it killed me.

Sure, I told myself I was still a writer, an Author. I kept up the façade I had created, and taught a few classes at a library, preaching about all the ways one can become a better writer. **Lesson One: Write. Write every day. Write your heart out, and bleed your soul onto the page.**

I needed that reminder. And encouragement. A cheerleader that understood all the ups and downs of the profession. I had/have my own fan club, a select few people who are supportive, and stand by me, and encourage me. But I needed more. I needed someone that truly understood, from the prospective only another writer can have, and I needed to ask for help.

Well, maybe I didn't outright ask for it, but this person, saw something in me. That creative edge. An ember of what used to be there, and was willing to help me figure out a way to reignite it. Reminding me of all the wonderful things that I love about writing and why I would be doing myself a disservice to just give up.

So this. What you're about to read, it all started with a friend. And a writing prompt.

That's right. Who knew? A silly writing prompt and that push I needed to just try. It was something so simple. Write about a writer who had lost their muse, and needed to figure out how to get it back.

I had to remind myself to start small. No pressure. To just let the prompt help me do the work. Allowing myself to capture my muse and bring it forth.

I think we, as writers, sometimes get overwhelmed by the big picture, the pressure to produce, to please, to entertain, and we forget, or begin to forget and let fade that creative spark that fills us and motivates us. I think, when writing truly begins to feel like a job, something you no longer look forward to doing when you wake up in the morning, and dread sitting at the keyboard, or lose that whisper from your muse, you need to step back. Take a breath. And remember what about writing you loved so much.

I love telling stories. I love the idea of entertaining other people. And with that friend, and that prompt, eventually leading to more prompts and more stories, and that faith and encouragement, I was reminded about all the good things about writing. Reminded about how awesome it feels to just let your heart and soul speak, creating characters, and writing prose.

In a way, a lot of the inspiration behind this collection of short stories is myself. That writer who lost their muse. Pieces of me are in every story. They are what helped me push forward, crumble that wall, and release some of my own inhibitions. Because with writing, sometimes you just have to change things up, too. And, boy, did I ever! This was an exploration of monumental proportions, and something totally new to me.

And I'm sure, now, some of you are wondering if I've recaptured my muse, again? Maybe not completely; but this, taking these stories, and entertaining people, and putting them out into the world, is a good start.

Madison Avery
June 2015

Luck be a Penny

RAYNE MCKAY rushed down the stairs, gripping the cool metal rail for support. She hurried, as best she could in a pair of stiletto heels, trying to reach the train before it pulled out of the station. She didn't want to be any later than she was already.

She was careful to shove people out of the way as nicely as she could, but as Rayne neared the platform, the train doors closed. A moment later, it was heading through the tunnel, disappearing out of sight. Rayne took a moment to catch her breath, uttering a few obscenities. There was no point in running anymore.

"Can you spare some change, ma'am?"

Looking to the ground, towards the voice she'd heard, Rayne saw a man. It wasn't an odd sight—not at the train station. There were always people lounging around, cups, signs or open guitar cases, hoping for coins, or better yet, a few crisp bills to land inside.

The odd thing about the homeless man was how Rayne's heart lurched, feeling sorry for him. Normally, she was the kind of person that would have walked on by, to the far end of the track, just to avoid him. Rayne hated that about herself. But she had been brought up with the belief that people could always find work, that being homeless was a choice. Of course, now she knew better, but Rayne couldn't help that they somehow made her more uncomfortable in her own skin than usual.

Rayne hadn't bothered to bring a purse with her. She hated them. She'd shoved her license and credit card into the back pocket of her jeans and her cell phone in the front as she rushed out the door that morning. But she found herself reaching into her pockets, anyway. Her hand plunged into each pocket, the ones in her pants, and next, the ones in her tweed coat, until she felt something.

When her hand pulled free and Rayne opened her palm, to her disappointment, there were a few crumpled gum wrappers, a used toothpick—gross, she thought with a blush—and one shiny penny.

"I'm sorry. This-this is all I have." She held out the copper coin, instantly wishing it could be more.

The man took the offering, closing his fingers around the coin. "It is what it is," he said. Then he took the coin, rested it on his thumb and flipped it in the air, catching it. "But you should keep it. A penny for your thoughts, and may it bring you good luck."

Rayne laughed, shaking her head. "Believe it or not, I'm not thinking anything. And I think life has given me all the luck it can. Please. Keep it. I insist."

An earnest smile spread over the man's face. "I think you're wrong. On both accounts. But I'll keep the penny."

With a nod and a warm smile of her own, Rayne turned to leave, just as another train pulled into the station. She found herself in the flow of passengers as they filed in. Rayne slumped into a seat by the window and gazed out, looking for the homeless man. When she searched the space, at the base of the stairs, against the wall, it was empty. He was gone. She didn't give the ordeal any more thought other than silently hoping the man would find some luck of his own, and a moment later, forgetting him completely.

When Rayne finally made it to the office of her literary agent, Lacy Brown, she was more than half an hour late. She opened the door slowly and walked in. There were piles of papers on the desk, on the floor, and overflowing the trash can. It was a wonder how such a disorganized person was so organized in matters of acquiring authors, and selling their works. She was one of the best. Rayne was thankful every day that Lacy had seen something within her early works and was confident in her skills as an up and coming author. That was six years ago, and five books later. But lately, Rayne was in a slump. In fact, the meeting she was late for was to discuss just that, she knew it.

"Come in, come in. I haven't got all day." Lacy waved her hand with a smile. She was short—five foot nothing—and the desk and papers overwhelmed her small stature. But her brown eyes and hair were warm and welcoming, which was a good facade for her. She was quite possibly the loudest, most obnoxious agent in the business, speaking open-heartedly, with little censor. As a meager peace offering, Rayne passed over one of the two Macchiatos she had wasted more time picking up on her way. Most days, Rayne was thankful she lived in the same bustling metropolis as her agent. It made it easier to get together to chat about upcoming works, deals, or their plans for the future. However, as of late, having to take the train and come to her office never meant anything good.

"Thanks. I suppose this is the least you could do." Lacy raised the cup in the air, in mock cheer, and took a tiny sip. She shivered. "Yummy." Then she set it on top of a stack of papers. "Sit down. We have lots to talk about."

Hesitantly, Rayne walked around the chair and plunked down. She wondered if she should start groveling now or wait. A silent beat or two passed, Lacy's eyes narrowed, lips pressed into a hard line. She pushed the bangs off her forehead, and Rayne shriveled under the scrutinizing stare.

"Rayne, what the fuck?" she finally spoke.

Ah, yes, there was the real Lacy Brown. Rayne shrugged and looked away. It was worse than sitting in the principal's office in high school. Sweat formed on her hands. Rayne rubbed them against her jeans, then fidgeted with frayed ends of the holes she'd paid for in the fabric.

"No, really. What. The. Fuck? You're late. Actually you're twice late because the publisher already gave you an extension. They're pissed. Hell, I'm pissed. You can see that, right? How pissed off I am?"

Meekly, Rayne replied, swallowing the lump in her throat. "Yes. I know. I can see it."

"No. I don't think you know the gravity of the situation we're both in. The publisher wants to see the first draft of the book in a month. Please, God, tell me you have something to give them. The entire world wants—no, needs—to know what happens to Clara and Dexter." Lacy stood from the desk and walked around, her eyes leveling with Rayne's. "And everyone wants to get paid. This is still a business."

With a deep inhale, Rayne said, "I'm sorry. I-I don't have it."

Lacy frowned. "It's been almost two years, Rayne, what's the problem?"

What was the problem? Rayne knew, from the moment Clara and Dexter materialized, how their epic love story would end. It was always meant to be a trilogy; that was how she'd pitched it to her agent, and how Lacy had sold it to the publisher, and now... Now, they hung in the air. She couldn't figure out how to get the words in her brain onto the page. She couldn't remember why she loved writing so much because now, it was a job. Rayne had lost sight of the bigger picture. It was all deadlines and book tours. Sure, she loved the money she'd made. Going from nearly destitute, to well-off, in the short span of two years. When her first series came out, hitting the bestseller charts immediately and becoming a hit, Rayne had almost become unstoppable.

But the fire that always fuelled her will to write had been extinguished, and now she owed her agent and publisher a book she didn't think she could ever write. Rayne was exhausted. Perhaps she'd risen too high, too fast, and this was the payback. She'd lost her muse, the voice in her head that helped paint the pictures to her novels, filling her with the confidence and words that needed to be written. It was gone.

"I-I don't know." Rayne exhaled the breath she'd been holding, and put her head in her hands. "I'm lost. It's lost."

"Oh, honey, nothing is ever truly lost," Lacy said, her high pitched voice taking on a soothing tone. "You just have to get back to it, and write. At this point, we'll take anything. Anything, Rayne, is better than nothing."

"Right. Okay. So, a month? Are you serious?" That wasn't good. At all. Most of the drafts Rayne had turned over had taken several. The fact that she hadn't even typed the opening line to the final installment of Clara and Dexter's book was a frightening thought.

"Am I ever not serious?" Lacy said, but her attention had shifted to the pile of crap on her desk. She fingered through some papers until she found what she wanted, turning back around towards Rayne. "Here." She held out a piece of paper. "I'm not a hand-holder, you know that, but this is a desperate time."

Rayne grabbed the page, but she would have sworn her eyes deceived her as she read. "This is the confirmation number to a flight?"

"And a hotel. I'm forcing you to take a vacation. You need it. Your book needs it. Different scenery might help spark something, and who knows, maybe you'll turn that book in ahead of the one-month deadline."

Overwhelmed, Rayne stood up and threw herself at her agent, hugging her tightly. Lacy was rigid, but a few seconds later, she relaxed and returned the gesture as best she could. "Thank you! I swear I can do this. I know I can."

"You don't have a choice, honey. If you don't turn in the novel, things are going to get ugly. And trust me, you haven't seen me ugly yet."

If that were true, Rayne definitely didn't want to see Lacy ugly. Even on her best day, Lacy was a force. Something told Rayne that if she couldn't turn in the book—well, that would most likely be the end of her career as an author. The pang she felt in her heart was the first emotion in a while that made her realize she wasn't ready to lose everything she'd spent years building. She had always aspired to be an author, and couldn't imagine doing anything else. It was just a dry spell. Writers had them all the time, and maybe Lacy was right, a trip, a change in scenery, and one hell of a deadline, was going to get her back on track. It had to.

After taking the train back to her neck of the woods, Rayne was still jittering with excitement. It had been years since she'd been on a vacation. She'd traveled, lots, but it was all in the name of "Authorly Duties." She had fun, sure. It was awesome to meet fans, sign books—that never seemed to get old—and mingle with fellow authors. They were always an interesting bunch and partied like there was no tomorrow. However, when she came home, usually more exhausted than when she left, she never felt like she had much time to herself to relax and enjoy the time away from home.

Walking the bustling streets, Rayne headed to her favorite grocery store. Sadly, she wouldn't be leaving for another two days, which meant she'd have to pick up a few things to get her through. She was a terrible cook; accidents often happened when she was in front of the stove. Mostly she relied on take-out, the microwave, or if need be, something she could toss in the oven. Something, of course, that wouldn't be burnt to a crisp too badly when the smoke alarm went off in her third-floor apartment because she'd forgotten about it.

There was a chill in the air, and Rayne pulled the lapels of her coat up in an effort to combat it. She rubbed her hands together and turned the corner, paying more attention to the concrete her heels clicked against than where she was walking.

What she heard first was a ringing sound. She couldn't place it—not right away—but it was something she recognized. On the tip of her tongue. But next, she was colliding with a stranger, stumbling backward. Her ass hit the concrete hard, and she yelped.

Rayne was eager to take the hand that was thrust in her face. She squinted her eyes, but the bright afternoon sun veiled the towering stranger before her, lacing the moment with intrigue. She felt the shudder of heat as soon as her hand slid into his, grasping it. It spread over her fingers and up her arm. It was an enticing feel. An effect she may have written about in her books, but never thought, ever, that it could be real. That instant connection with someone that spreads over you, jolting you awake.

She let the firm grasp help haul her upright. It lingered for a second, before the warmth faded away, as soon as she pulled back, brushing her curled hair out of her eyes.

Though she hadn't meant it, a gasp pushed through her parted lips when she realized who had helped her up.

It was the homeless man from the morning, and now she was suddenly facing him.

"I'm sorry, ma'am. I wasn't... Lucky Penny?"

The blush that spread over Rayne was fast and burned hot. "Yeah. I'm sorry, I wasn't watching where I was going, either."

A second later, Rayne heard the ringing sound. A sort of metallic ping as the homeless man flipped the penny she had given him earlier, into the air, catching it. "Seems you should have kept this, after all," he said.

Rayne replied, "I'm a klutz, and wasn't paying attention. Lack of luck had nothing to do with it."

It was then she took a step back, taking a moment to let her eyes appraise the man. He was dressed well enough, not exactly what you'd expect from a man hoping for a handout. Blue jeans, a warm–looking, gray wool sweater. They weren't tattered or dirty, and Rayne was sure the delightful smell of woodiness and citrus fruit rolled into one was emanating from him. Her deliberate stare swept up his length and to his eyes, which grabbed her attention further. They were, after all, no matter how cliché, the window to the soul.

This man's eyes were spellbinding. Composed of scratches of malachite; a luminescent green Rayne had never seen before, but wanted to commit the precious gemstone-like appearance to memory. They swallowed her up with an intense gaze she couldn't seem to break away from.

Rayne didn't need to look at the rest of him. It was not necessary. His eyes were warm, and sincere, a touch of mystery within the green. They were honest. She could tell. And she was immediately taken with them.

"Maybe, maybe not." He flipped the coin in the air again, snapping Rayne back. "But this time, you were thinking something. What was it? You'd been biting your lip, gnawing on it like it was a light afternoon snack."

Finding a laugh to share was easy; he was funny. Though she hadn't realized she'd been biting her lips. Impulsively, she wiped a hand across her mouth, her fingers drawing back a smear of crimson blood.

What had she been thinking? About the vacation, for sure. Yet, that wasn't all. It was about the rock that had plummeted in her stomach, weighing her down with doubts, already, about whether or not she could turn over a complete manuscript in less than a month. When she'd left Lacy's office, she had been confident. However, as the minutes began to tick away, so did that confidence, replaced by an overwhelming uncertainty. Rayne had no idea where to start.

She shrugged in reply, looking away. "I have a deadline. A big one. Important. Actually, almost life or death, but I just—I just don't think I can meet it."

The man did something that surprised Rayne. He reached towards her and rested his fingers under her chin, urging her to look up at him. "You can do it. I know you can." Her eyes fluttered closed as his warm, minty breath washed over her causing Rayne's heart to pitch forward.

For Rayne, the delicate touch, and his earnest words didn't last log enough. She heard the flip of his penny, and when she opened her eyes, he was gone.

She rushed up the street and down, searching for the man who'd given her the most sincere moment of her life. Though he knew nothing of who she was, she believed with all her heart he had indeed meant what he'd said. That she could do it. No matter how insignificant it was, knowing someone else knew that, started a few ideas to flitter through her brain.

* * *

17

As Rayne sat in the window seat of the airplane, she used the short flight to get to work, and typed on her laptop. She thought back, often, to the moment on the street with the homeless man, her emotions tingling. He had given her the tiniest spark towards getting back that urge to write. It came unexpectedly, but Rayne grasped at the few ideas with open arms. She'd spent the better part of the last two days plotting out Clara and Dexter's final book. But to her dismay, the ember began to fade. The longer she looked at the computer, the more she realized what she had written down was crap. She knew it. It wasn't the epic final installment her readers deserved.

Although she didn't select the words and delete them, Rayne let out a frustrated grumble and closed the lid on her laptop with more force than needed. Taking the small plastic cup of rye and coke, she slung it back, letting the burn of the alcohol slide down her throat. She'd felt as though she'd wasted the last couple days, the deadline looming.

Pressing her head against the rest, she closed her eyes, bringing her hands up and over, shielding them further from the glow of the plane.

Rayne heard the tell-tale sound of a thumb connecting with a metallic coin being propelled through the air. It was faint but clear. She'd now recognize the sound anywhere. Pulling her hands from her face, she looked to her left, across the aisle. Then she wiggled in her chair, got to her knees and peered over her seat, looking front and back, searching out the sound.

"Ma'am, we're about to make our descent. I need you to sit down and buckle up," a flight attendant said, coming down the aisle.

"Did you see... I mean, is there a man on the plane, really tall, handsome-looking, flipping a coin in the air?" Rayne was still searching the faces of the passengers she could see. Oddly enough, she hoped she would find him, but when the flight attendant shook her head, she slid back down into her seat. Her hand rested on her heart, feeling the erratic beats within. It was strange. Of course, he wouldn't be on her flight. He was probably back at the train station, begging for change. Rayne had apparently misinterpreted the sound she'd heard.

* * *

After checking in and dropping off her luggage in her room, Rayne went into the lobby of the hotel. She was used to eating alone, and found a cozy corner in the lounge to enjoy a meal and a glass of burgundy merlot. She still hadn't felt the inkling to write, and may have drowned a little of her woes in one too many glasses of wine. Rayne didn't care. She was, after all, on vacation. There was no one there to scold her for being tipsy, there were no fans that expected her to be this brilliant and creative author. She was all by herself, which most times, Rayne preferred.

After finishing her meal, gulping down the dregs of her wine, instead of heading back up to her room, Rayne went into the lobby and headed out the doors. She was staying in a cozy seaside community, and with the impending sunset approaching, Rayne thought a beautiful sight like that might re-spark the ideas that still floated in her mind. She really did need to figure out a way to just... collect all the thoughts in one cohesive weave and get to work.

For the most part, the only thing holding Rayne back was herself and the fear of failure.

As she walked along the boardwalk, the lapping waves of the ocean just below her, what seemed to work, sort of, was taking her mind off the novel and to just be... Rayne spent more time looking at the sights, how many people still covered the sandy beach, playing in the water, screaming and laughing. Carefree. The shops and bars across from the ocean were bustling with activity. Sitting on a bench, Rayne people-watched; often times one of her favorite activities. She found that going unnoticed was a great way to see how people truly interacted. Many of her characters in the past had been created by something she had seen.

An older couple held hands, clinging to each other; such love swirling between their gazes. A mother, holding a small baby, cooing. She looked exhausted, dark circles around her eyes, and yet, as she looked down at the little person, all that didn't seem to matter. The look of adoration in her eyes was compelling. A young couple stopped abruptly, and the guy grabbed his companion's hand, pulling her into a small alcove between the buildings. Pressing her against the wall, he kissed her passionately, as though they were the only two people in the world.

And that's how life should be. Always. That love, that transcends all things, making it as though there is nothing else that matters. Just the deep, consuming feeling of giving yourself over completely to another. Rayne wished she had that. That she could reach out and take that kind of love and shove it into her story.

Dexter and Clara needed it too. She had put them through the ringer, left their love story hanging, wide-open, with gaping holes, and tearing them from each other. Only she knew they would end up back in each other's arms. It was inevitable. She just had to write it.

After a long while, Rayne began to retrace her steps, heading back towards the hotel. She felt lighter, more relaxed but still not sure she could put pen to paper, yet. The other problem she'd been having about Dexter and Clara was the simple fact they needed a love story ending that would give justice for what they'd gone through. Rayne wasn't sure how to do that, when she had never experienced that all-consuming love herself. She had never given her heart to someone freely. She guarded it. Always. Only, at times, giving small pieces of herself away. How was she to write about something she'd never experienced before?

The ringing sound was abrupt, slicing through the air, reaching her ears. Rayne looked to her left, right, forward and backward. She knew, this time without a doubt, it was the sound of the man flipping her penny in the air. Picking up her pace, Rayne ran. A silly sensation in her heart propelled her forward.

Then, there, sitting just outside the doors of the hotel, she saw him. At least, she thought she did. She blinked her eyes a few times in amazement and then concern. She hated that she knew seeing him again, hours away from the city, should have brought on a more instant reaction—she should have been scared. Yet, she wasn't. She was oddly comforted by the sight, no matter how peculiar it was.

"Are you stalking me?" Rayne came up to him. "Should I be calling the cops?" It was an honest question that deserved an answer. She placed her hands on her hips, toe-tapping against the ground.

"Lucky Penny, fancy meeting you here."

She shook her head. "No. Not fancy. You-you shouldn't be here." But she found herself stepping to the side of him, turning and sliding her back against the wall, sitting next to him. She brought her legs up and hugged them. "Who are you?" she whispered.

"Would you believe me if I said I was here because you needed me?"

Rayne scoffed. He flipped the coin in the air again, but before he could catch it, she snatched it out the air. "No. I wouldn't. I would start to think you're crazy. Or I'm crazy. That this moment isn't real. It's not actually happening. Because it doesn't make sense. At all."

The man put his hand over top of Rayne's as she still held the coin in her palm. "Why does it have to make sense? Why can't you just let the moment happen? Is it because deep down you know it's what you need?" But Rayne wasn't sure she'd heard him, not entirely. She had been concentrating on the sensation in her hand. His skin was soft, warm, and that tingle of electricity was back.

Pushing away the awe, she stumbled over her words but replied, "How do you know what I need?"

"Because I felt it. More than once. You've been asking yourself questions, and I'm here, Rayne, to give you a taste of the answers."

Hearing her name roll off his tongue shot a tidal wave of emotion through her. It shouldn't have. Her heart was betraying her in the sense that she knew the entire exchange between the two was wrong. "How-how do you know my name?"

"The same way that I know if you dig deep and relax, you'll know mine, too."

No matter how absurd that was, Rayne did as he'd said. She closed her eyes, tuned out everything she could, and listened. Listened to what her heart or her mind, or the crazy voices that often took residence in her brain, were trying to tell her.

At first, the only the sound she heard was of her own deep breaths. The thump of her heart. The blood rushing through her veins. The more she surrendered, desperate to hear something, the more she swore she heard. A delicate whisper, a nudge to keep searching. She pushed aside the millions of ideas clouding her mind, ideas begging to be written that she'd never had the will to write, and then, it came. Sort of a funny taste on her tongue. A vibration through her veins. Until the information she wanted could be plucked from her mind. She wrapped imaginary fingers around it, gripping it tightly, clinging to the sensation it gave her.

"Cole," she whispered so quietly she hadn't been sure he heard her.

She pulled his hand to hers, lacing their fingers together, the penny trapped between them. Rayne stood and tugged at him, silently pleading with her eyes. Cole exhaled a breath and stood, nearly pressing his chest against hers. The feel of his body so close ignited within her a moment of pleasure that tickled her stomach.

"Come with me. Please," she said, already pulling him towards the hotel.

Cole trailed behind, but his long strides matched to her shorter ones as they walked side by side through the lobby.

Knowing what she needed made the whole idea for Rayne easier to accept. He'd been right. She'd been asking questions, for months. It was always her biggest struggle. She needed someone to come and take away the block in her mind, allow her the chance to write again. It wasn't quite simply writer's block she suffered from, it was more. It was the question she'd asked herself as she walked back to the hotel, the same thing she'd been thinking when she'd lied to Cole the first time they met.

Rayne always believed that part of her couldn't finish Dexter and Clara's story because she didn't know how to give them what they needed. Connect them completely in a way she'd never experienced. And maybe her chance was here. Sort of.

Once in the elevator, Rayne boldly stepped towards Cole. She closed the final inches of distance between them. "I need you. I need you take it away. To give me—" But she didn't finish. Instead, she leaned up on her tiptoes and placed her lips against his. Soft and careful, but when Cole's arms wrapped around her waist, forcing her closer, the kiss became more urgent.

Suddenly, her hands were everywhere, exploring him. She touched his face, the tips of her fingers scratching the stubble on his jaw. Rayne dragged her hands over his spine, and back up his chest. Cole did the same, smoothing his palms over her. In one swift motion, he'd grabbed her by the hips, lifting her from the ground. He turned, pressing Rayne against the wall of the elevator.

With Cole's hands on either side of her head, he took her bottom lip into his mouth. He sucked and nibbled before moving to kiss her cheek, the tip of her nose, the lobe of her ear. One of his hands left its place, sliding down her torso, and gripped the underside of her thigh, pulling her leg up, desperate to close any remaining gaps between them.

"Cole," Rayne murmured as she felt his erection pressing through his jeans, teasing her in just the right spot. He rubbed against her, causing a savory quiver between her legs, her core tingling at the sensation.

They broke apart when the elevator stopped and the doors opened on Rayne's floor. Cole captured her hand with his and the two walked, with wide smiles, out and down the hallway.

Rayne had never felt so exhilarated in her life. She was the shy girl, always, and never would have imagined she would be so eager to get someone into her bed. Yet, here she was, casting fervent looks in Cole's direction. Her mind hadn't completely wrapped around the situation, and she didn't dare put too much thought into it. It didn't really matter if Cole was simply a manifestation of her brain, or if he was real, and he'd known just what she needed. If he could somehow pull the wedge in her mind free, she was all the better off. She would deal with the aftermath later—maybe never—because right here, right now, Rayne was desperate with the idea of having Cole. Nothing else mattered.

"Where's your key?"

"In-in my pocket," Rayne said. She went to get it, but Cole's hand was on her bum, hand in the pocket of her jeans. He squeezed, which caused her to giggle as he pulled the card free.

In a hoarse voice, he said, "And the room number?"

Using a shaky gesture, she pointed down to the end of the hall. "It's the last one."

The two picked up their pace until Cole was shoving the card into the slot. He jiggled it around, with a groan, until the light turned green and he was able to push the door open. They practically fell into each other's arms, through the threshold, the door being kicked shut by Cole's boot.

"I-I don't normally do this," Rayne said. "Never, actually. Ever." But Cole pushed his finger over her lips, shushing her.

"That doesn't matter, as long as you're sure this is what you want."

Rayne didn't have to think about it. Not at all. She craved the release she anticipated, both mentally and physically. "It is. I'm sure."

"Then anything that happens is because we want it to."

Biting her lip, Rayne nodded, reaching for his sweater, curling her fingers into the fabric as she pulled it up and over Cole's head. Letting go, it fell in a heap on the floor, but her hands found the swath of rich black hair on his head. She pulled her fingers through it, leaning closer to him, kissing across his chest. It was sprinkled with hair, and it tickled her nose until she swirled a circle around his hardened nipple with her tongue. At the motion, Cole grabbed her hips again, a low groan coming from deep within his throat.

The sound enticed her with another amplified shiver, and she pulled back.

"I want you," Cole said as he reached for the belt on her coat, yanking it open. He moved fast as he pulled the buttons loose, and then slid the fabric over her arms. But he didn't stop there. He wrenched the fabric of her shirt up, pulling it over her head. Next, he took the elastic that had tied her curls in place and snapped it free.

Her hair spilled over her bare shoulders, resting in length just above the cups of her green satin bra. "Exquisite," he whispered, his gaze on her breasts that swelled with each breath of air she took in. He fingered the fabric, dipping below the cup, teasing her nipple.

She moaned at the delicate touch, slowly coming undone with the need to have him completely. To feel him inside her.

"Come here. Come with me," he said, pulling her towards the bathroom.

It was a grand space, a huge tub, double-wide shower, granite floors and marble vanity. Lacy had spared no expense when she picked the hotel for Rayne, and briefly, she wondered what she would have thought had she known what Rayne was up to. Knowing Lacy, Rayne knew she'd be the one cheering her on, telling her to go for it. To let go of any lingering reservations she might have.

Cole pulled at the button on her jeans and gradually eased the fly open. The sound echoed throughout the space as he took the moment further by slipping his hands down and over her backside. He gripped her tightly but then pushed his hands even lower until he'd pulled her pants to the floor. Cole then kneeled in front of her. Rayne lifted up her foot, letting him remove her heels, one at time. He gave her toes a gentle massage. Who knew something so simple could feel so good, Rayne wondered, trying to beg with her eyes for more. Instead, he smiled back, leaning towards her, kissing each of her knees.

His kisses trailed up one leg and over her hipbone, across her torso and navel, and down the other. But where Rayne really wanted to be kissed, where all the feelings inside her were concentrated, was the one place he seemed to be avoiding. If only to tease her further.

He had to have known what she wanted. Rayne wanted to break the silence and tell him. Tell him she wanted more, but she didn't trust her voice. She may have seemed assertive, but in reality, she was far from it. She settled for the only thing she could. Rayne opened her mouth and said, "Please." It was all she could manage and was more of a moan than a word. But Cole took the request—a challenge, perhaps—as he peppered kisses back over her torso and down the front of her panties, sliding them down.

She wasn't bare, but thankful she had kept herself neatly trimmed as Cole took his hand and pushed her legs further apart. Rayne closed her eyes as he pressed his palm against her core, and then slipped a finger between her, rubbing slow and deliberate circles around her clitoris.

Rayne's breath hitched as she felt herself begin to swell, wetness slicking his finger. She placed her hands on his shoulders, digging her nails into his shoulders, forcing herself to stay upright.

Her knees wobbled as Cole said, "Can I taste you, Rayne?" And she opened her eyes in time to see him take his finger, rub it over his lips, and then slip it into his mouth. "Delicious," he hummed with a smile of undeniable admiration.

At the sight before her, Rayne shuddered, her entire body becoming rigid as an orgasm took over fast and abrupt, a sensation that had her nearly falling over. She blushed profusely, barely able to look Cole in the eyes. He'd barely touched her, and yet, she was overwhelmed.

"Mmm. You look beautiful when you come. I'd very much like to see that expression again."

Rayne gulped in a breath of air. She nodded, as another build-up of pressure had already begun to take control of her. Cole stood and kissed the grin from her face before pulling back and turning his attention to the shower. He turned the lever and sent a spray of water to spill from the showerhead. He kicked off his boots, taking the time to slip his pants off, revealing a pair of black boxers. His very evident erection sprang free from its confines as he pulled them down, lastly removing his socks.

Cole's hard-on was impressive, and Rayne couldn't imagine what it would feel like to have it inside her, gorging her.

"Are you coming?"

For a second, Rayne didn't understand the question. She blinked a few times. Not yet, she thought with a smile, but then realized he had stepped into the shower and was beckoning her to follow his lead. She was quick to reach behind and unclasp her bra, the remaining article that stood between them. Cole reached for her hand

and helped her in. She shivered as the warm water rushed over her cool skin, causing her nipples to tighten. "I'd like to wash you, Rayne. Would that be okay?" "Yes. Please. Touch me," she exhaled.

Cole was leisure in his movements as he lathered a loofa with soap, and then gently smoothed it over Rayne's skin. He started with her arms, one at a time, and then her legs. He turned her around, concentrating on her back and her bottom. There he was, teasing her again, avoiding the only areas she truly wanted to feel his touch.

When Cole reached up and cupped both of Rayne's breasts in his hands, having discarded the soapy loofa, she whimpered. He pressed his erection against her back, and kissed the curves of her neck as he pinched and teased her nipples. She couldn't take much more, she knew, and craned her head over her shoulder. He crushed his lips against hers, holding her in place. One hand traveled to her neck, the other skimmed over her, all the way down, until he buried his finger inside her. Rayne let out a muffled cry, relishing in the delightful feel as he thrust in and out of her, the water and her ever-growing wetness providing the right amount of lubricant.

He broke their kiss and whispered in her ear. "You can come for me again. I know you want to."

Though she knew she didn't need his permission, she tensed at his words, as his thumb rubbed against her swollen clit until it was too much. Rayne couldn't hold the climax at bay, and instead, let it take over. Cole stilled his movements, palming her, letting her ride out her orgasm.

"Mmm. I think it's my turn," Rayne said. She turned and dropped to her knees and took him into her hand. Carefully she moved her grasp up and down the length of his hard, yet soft, erection. She did that for a few minutes as Cole thrust his fingers into the wet strands of her hair. When she had worked up more courage, she leaned in and placed her mouth over the tip and teased him with her lips. A moment later, she drew as much of his length into her mouth as she could, sucking and swirling her tongue. Cole groaned and pulled on her hair. Eventually, she felt him swell inside her mouth, and she knew she had a quick decision to make. But when she opened her eyes and saw that he was staring intensely at her, the jade of them showed her more love than she could have expected. She needed to do this for him, and so she sucked harder, faster, adding her hand to the rhythm of her sliding mouth and twirling tongue, until she felt his release. It was warm and salty, and she swallowed, sucking every last drop that he eased into her mouth.

The whisper of the story Rayne knew she was supposed be working on grew loud in her ears as she lay on the bed, Cole before her. She would have never thought it possible but she knew, without a doubt, that he was crumbling her writer's block. In turn, infusing her with the lust and desire she knew she needed in order to create Dexter and Clara's novel. She wasn't ready to let go of

Cole or the night, yet. There were still pieces of the puzzle that were eluding her and she hoped that as Cole continued to ravage her, they would become clearer.

Cole was hovering over her, kissing her lips, sweetly, his tongue asking permission to enter her mouth. She parted and found her own tongue was just as eager. He tasted of mint, still, and she loved how his kisses were soft. He seemed to be pouring into them all the passion he could, making sure she knew what the moment meant to him.

"I want you inside me," she said through a moan as his pressed against her, on the cusp of melding their bodies together. "Please."

Lifting up, Cole grinned. He rolled back on his heels sitting upright, and then, he lifted Rayne's hips, and guided her towards him, wrapping her legs around his torso.

"I missed that expression last time. I won't miss it again."

Cole lightly pressed into her. She gasped and gripped the sheets in her hands, arching her back towards him. He waited a second, slid himself out, only to push in deeper with the next thrust, his hands still pressed tightly to her hips. But as he continued the motion, he pulled her breast into his hand, squeezing it with just the right amount of pressure, as he rolled her nipple between his fingers.

The moment, for Rayne, wasn't going to last long as he was able to push himself deep within her. Teasing her breasts only heightened her arousal even more.

What threw her into a frenzy were his fingers sliding down, engaging her further as he caressed her most responsive spot. Heat boiled her blood, as electricity sizzled through her veins. It clutched her heart, burned her lungs, and then, all at once, she felt the onslaught of the most demanding orgasm she'd ever felt. It carried her over the edge. She cried out, yet forced her eyes to stay open. Locked on Cole. So they could be wrapped up in each other completely. He didn't turn away, not even when his movements became erratic, forceful. He grunted, pounding into her. Rayne felt herself clench tightly around his throbbing erection. They rode the last waves of their climax together, sweat glistening their skin, breaths coming fast and shallow.

Lying in each other's arms, Cole said, "That's what they need. They need to be devoted to each other. You need to give them that obsessive lust, their ultimate desires."

Consumed by exhaustion, Rayne mumbled something incoherent as Cole squeezed her tighter. She knew what they needed. She'd been beating around the bush with their attraction and need for each other through two books. Rayne had brought Clara to Dexter when he was wounded and incapable of loving her back. He'd walked away in the first book. But Clara hadn't given up in the second. She knew what she wanted. And though the timing wasn't right for their epic love, it

34

was time now. They were better off together than they were apart.

The novel Rayne had been worried about writing finally had a storyline. She now knew what it was like to be in love with the idea of the perfect romance. Though she knew this moment with Cole wouldn't last, she at least felt utterly satisfied with how it turned out. He had done just what she'd needed. He somehow took away the block in her brain and opened up her heart.

Maybe she hadn't been able to give Clara and Dexter the happy ending they deserved because she didn't know how. She'd never had her own. Never felt bliss in a way that still ached between her legs and plagued her heart with the need for more. That was part of what love was.

"Thank you," Rayne said. She tried to fight off the sleep that beckoned her, not wanting her perfect night with Cole to end. "You took it away. I feel, for the first time, that I could get up and write a dozen pages without a thought."

"I didn't do anything. Not really. You were the one blocking yourself and your emotions. I just helped you to let go of them."

"Mmm," she said. "You're real, right? Not just my imagination?"

Kissing her temple, Cole said, "I'm as real as you want me to be."

It wasn't the answer Rayne wanted, but she knew that sometimes the muse, the whisper that helps with the stories, comes from all things. For some, it's a beautiful picture hung on the wall of a museum. Others hear it in the words of a song, the melody flowing the ideas they need. For Rayne, her ultimate muse came from a man she didn't know completely but fell for deeply. He became the whisper that continued to weave together the end of her love story. And was the last voice she heard when sleep finally pulled her in.

That, and the sound of a penny whistling through the air.

* * *

When Rayne woke in the morning, her body hurt, but in all the right places. She didn't mind. She remembered what had caused the ache between her legs and smiled. She'd fallen asleep in Cole's arms, feeling his heart beat against her back, his warm breath over her skin.

But when she rolled over, he was gone.

"Cole?" She called out, but when she sat up and saw the shiny penny left on the nightstand, she knew he wouldn't reply. There was a messily scrawled note, and Rayne pick it up, holding it between her fingers as she pushed away the need to well with tears, the loss she felt. She knew her time with Cole had a deadline, just like the novel she had to write.

Rayne,
A penny for your thoughts and good luck
along the way.
Yours,
Cole

Rayne clutched the note to her heart, the penny in her hand. She stared at the empty hotel room for a few minutes before she gathered her wits and slipped from the bed. Not bothering to get dressed, the sheet her only cover, she sat at the desk and pulled out her computer. She began to write, Cole's voice guiding her forward, helping her decide the twists and turns Clara and Dexter needed to take. She poured everything she felt into the manuscript, drawing her own emotions forward and letting them slip through her fingers, into the keys she pressed.

* * *

By the end of Rayne's week in the sleepy ocean-side town, she had produced what she was sure was her best manuscript yet. She felt proud and knew the story had always been there, she just needed the courage to write it down. As it turned out, one night where she forgot it all and got caught up in a little romance of her own, was just what she needed. It broke down the imaginary walls and released the muse within.

The thud the manuscript made on Lacy's desk was liberating.

Lacy looked from the pages to Rayne, amazed. "How the hell—"

"Seems I just needed a vacation."

But Lacy saw through Rayne. She knew. "No, what you needed was a good fuck. You're always wound up so tight. But whatever. I don't care how it happened. I'm just... Shit. I can't wait to read it."

"It's the impressive conclusion that Dexter and Clara deserve," Rayne said with a smile.

"Great. Should we talk about a spin-off? There's whispers that Grant and Leah's story should be told next. Have any ideas?"

Rayne closed her eyes. They were the best friends of the main characters she had spent the last several years with, and to her delight, she could hear her muse, Cole, murmuring in her ear. "Maybe. But I just got back from vacation. And wrote an entire manuscript in a week, how many of your authors have done that?"

"Just you, honey, just you."

When Rayne left the building, she took the penny from her pocket and rested it on her thumb. Though she wasn't nearly as talented, she was able to flip the lucky penny in the air and catch it before putting it back into her pocket for safe keeping.

Tires screeched, and the sound of a horn wailed through the air. Rayne looked up. Across the street stood a man, tall, and from here she knew he had the most enchanting green eyes she'd ever seen. She smiled. He winked. When she refocused, he was gone.

But like the penny in her pocket, and the voice in her head, she knew that wasn't going to be the last she saw of him. He would always be as real to her as she wanted him to be.

Dances with Muses

MOLLY WAITED patiently for her boyfriend, Ryan, to pass out. When he had come home from work, temper flaring, she was all too happy to pop the top off a beer and hand it to him. In fact, she was the perfect girlfriend and brought him cold beer after cold beer, just to keep him content. It was better he drowned himself in the frothy amber ale, staring for hours at the TV, than turning his attention and residual anger he felt after a hard day's work, on her.

She didn't think she could take one more night of his shit. Molly had put up with a lot over the years with the hope that he'd get better. Appreciate her more. Become the boyfriend she was sure—at times—she deserved. But most love stories are a lie. Real life is never like that. And Molly was trapped. Making excuses for him time and time again.

Once in a while, she'd see the glimmer of the man he used to be, still there. Ryan would show up with a bouquet of flowers; a new notebook wrapped in fancy paper, complete with a bow. Sometimes he took Molly out dancing—though usually that kind of night started out well but ended with his fist in some guy's face. But he had tried. Most times, that was all she expected of him.

Things could always be worse, and Molly knew that. So she took those moments, no matter how fleeting, and held them close. She knew you couldn't change a man, but that didn't stop her from hoping.

On the nights when things got particularly bad; when he'd taken to breaking a lamp, or tossing a dish on the floor, or grabbing at her in a way that made her feel cheap, she wrote. Aspiring author wasn't the right word. As she knew, most of what she penned in her notebooks, or typed out in a document, hidden deep within her hard drive, was really only meant for her.

She lacked the confidence to make something of the tales she'd begun to invent. That might have been some of Ryan's doing; saying she'd been silly to think it was anything more than a hobby. An author had to have graduated from high school—Molly hadn't, having dropped out before she got her cap and gown. Writers needed a college education—Molly had taken a few courses, after getting her GED, but couldn't seem to make it stick. That also might have had something to do with Ryan, who couldn't manage her away from the house for more than a few hours. He was fiercely over-protective. After the fourth or fifth time of him creating a scene outside the doors of the evening classes she was taking, Molly was so embarrassed she could never bring herself to go back. Ryan had also told her an author had to be good, that what they wrote had to be entertaining. She'd made the mistake, one time, of sharing with him a few stories she'd produced. She'd been excited, proud, and feeling over the moon at having created something worth sharing. However, Ryan read, frowned and criticized. For a time, she let him shatter any thought she might have had about being any good. She hadn't been willing to give up that easily. Instead, waiting until he was asleep or passed out, or not even home, before she pulled out her laptop and began to write, keeping it hidden.

As it were, the more she wrote, the more she loved it. Molly had begun to crave the release it gave her. An outlet for all the disappointment in her life. She'd be the first to admit she'd made a few wrong turns along the way, which added to her unhappiness and feeling of not ever being able to do better. Because as Ryan criticized her story, he had done the same to her, over and over again. She'd felt worthless; even more, she believed she wasn't desirable to anyone but him. There would never be another man in her life who would put up with her quirks, financially support her, and love her. If what Ryan truly felt was adoration. Convenience, maybe. But love? She couldn't imagine why someone who supposedly felt that way would treat her so poorly. And yet, she was no better. Because she still found, when she dug deep, that she loved Ryan, at least a little bit.

That all changed, though, when Molly discovered she could adore someone else, more intensely, all consuming. She cherished the characters she brought into existence. And she treasured—even more—that she could develop and create the perfect man. She could put herself into the stories she wrote, and give herself the knight she deserved. Give herself all the things that were missing.

It happened late one night, tears blurring her vision as she stared at a blank page. Most of the stories, until that point, were fluffy tales of adventure. She hadn't yet broached the subject of realism or romance. She'd only dabbled. But a voice came to her; told Molly to wipe away the tears she'd been shedding and type.

Molly was hesitant. Unsure. But as the muse inside her—the one that spoke to her softly, lulling her with his voice—created a picture, she couldn't help but be excited. He had materialized out of thin air, but soon became the central character—the handsome man—in all her latest works. Because of what he could offer her, that escape had begun to turn into so much more.

Soon, Molly spent every waking minute—when Ryan wasn't around—with her muse. Her character. He had given himself a name and declared it to her. Atticus. No longer just a name or a whisper; he'd become more. Atticus was tall, towering over Molly. She loved how she had to look up, within the story, to see his eyes. They were multifaceted; a deep cognac color, fragmented with rays of green expanding from dark pupils. Though he changed a little with each story she put him in, his features were always the same. Kissable lips. A smile that spread wide, flashing her with perfectly shaped teeth and a swath of soft, light brown hair that curled around his ears. He had different careers, cars, favorite songs or beloved pets, but what he stood for, and how he felt about Molly, was always the same. He was gentle. Thoughtful. He was devoted to making Molly happy, and often times would sweep her into a story of unforgettable romance. Atticus knew all her desires, and he was able to please her in every way. He'd take her on journeys, not just of different locales, but of exploring each other's souls. He was everything to her, and her, him.

Atticus became so real, so immediate in Molly's life, that while he told her what to write, she felt as though he could hear her too. He had turned into more than just a muse. He was a friend, a lover, and the two became so entwined that the lines of reality, for Molly, had begun to blur. It became almost impossible for her to distinguish what was part of the story and what was part of real life.

"I think we should go swimming," Molly said to Atticus. He was standing on the edge of the beach, water lapping at his toes.

He turned towards her, with that smile that lit up his eyes and warmed her heart. "It's cold," he replied, leaning down, scooping sand into his hand, only to let it slip through his fingers.

"It doesn't have to be."

Atticus shook his head. "No, it doesn't have to be. We could go somewhere warmer. Just you and me."

Molly looked around. The beach was barren. Footsteps in the sand were the only indication there had been others. But now it was only Atticus at the shoreline and Molly lazing under an umbrella. The wind was cool, causing a shiver to spread goose bumps over her mostly bare, bikini-clad body.

"It is just you and I. It always is."

"I wish that were true." His voice took on a somber tone, emotion filling his eyes. She raised her eyebrows, a silent question playing on her lips. "You're still with him."

"With who?"

"I want you all to myself, Molly. I hate having to share you. To share you with him."

"You're not sharing me. Not really. This is as real as it gets. This is where I always want to be. With you. I only go back to the other place because I have to."

Atticus let out a sigh, gripping the back of his neck. "So where should we go?"

When Molly stilled her typing fingers, she was pulled back. She felt herself gasp as she took in her surroundings. She half expected to still be on the beach, the breeze fluttering Atticus' open shirt. Only she wasn't. She was in her room, blankets thrown over her body, pillows propping her up against her headboard. The computer poised in her lap, and the cursor on the screen blinking, waiting for her to answer Atticus' question.

"Where do you want to go?" she asked aloud.

From within her mind, Atticus whispered, "The ocean. You should pack a bag, and buy a one-way ticket."

Molly laughed, but it was strained. "I can't. I have work. And a life here," she said, a little disappointed.

"You could have a life with me."

That was absurd. She already had a life with Atticus. He knew her better than anyone because he was a figment of her imagination. But that didn't stop her, if only for a second, from wondering what it would be like. To be with Atticus, forever.

"I can't. Not really. But we can go to the ocean. Just you and I. We can swim in the crystal blue waters of Fiji. We can lay in the sand and make love under the stars..." She felt Atticus within. Though she knew he wasn't entirely satisfied, he began to utter the words she needed to type. The ones that would whisk her to Fiji, if only for a little while.

* * *

Something banged in the hallway outside the door and Molly bolted up. She tried to shake the images of crystal water and sandy paths twisting through jungles out of her mind. She turned to the clock above her desk. "Shit. How'd it get so late so quick?"

"Molly!" Ryan's voice had a slur to it, still drunk from the countless beers she'd offered him. "Where are you, you bitch?"

Another bang and something smashed to the hardwood floors—a photograph from the wall, Molly guessed. Quickly, she saved her Fiji escapade and closed the lid on her computer, only to shove it under her bed. She messed up the pillows and covers and threw herself against them, eyes closing. It took everything inside her to slow her breathing and steady her heart. Perhaps he'd just fall into bed, clothes still on, and be snoring loudly a few minutes later...

The door to the bedroom flung open with so much force it banged against the wall, the sound like a crack of lightning that shook the walls and blasted loud in her ears. Molly couldn't pretend to be asleep anymore. It scared her with a jolt, causing her heart to race violently in her chest.

"What are you doing?" he grunted, framed by the door and a small ray of light from the kitchen. It gave him a sinister appearance, rather than an ethereal one.

Molly steeled herself, stretched her arms up and yawned quietly. She rubbed fake sleep from her eyes and said, "Sleeping."

Ryan was disgruntled with the answer. Eyes narrowed, muttering a curse, he stepped further into the room, looking around in hope of finding her up to something. He looked in the closet. He wrenched open the curtains, checking the latch on the window. Next, Ryan went to bend down as if to look under the bed.

Molly was quick to grab his attention by asking, "What are you doing?" Uneasiness clenching her stomach.

He brought himself upright. "I heard voices. Who were you talking to?" He turned towards her, square shoulders, arms on his hips, and chest puffed out.

"No-no one." But that hadn't been true. Out of the corner of her eye, she swore she could see Atticus in the reflection of her vanity mirror. His head downcast with sadness. "I was just sleeping. Maybe a bad dream?"

Ryan let out an annoyed huff, but his features had begun to relax. He took a step closer to the bed and began stripping. Molly wanted to avert her eyes. He was already aroused, maybe by the power he knew he had over her, or maybe the late night TV switched to something a little more 18A. It didn't matter. He was quick to put his hands on her after sliding the covers back and getting into bed.

Molly resisted the urge to cringe as Ryan groped her, pressing his hardness into her side.

"Why are you still wearing clothes?" he grunted, tugging at the flimsy barrier between them.

She'd settled down to write in a pair of boy-shorts and a tank top. Hardly considered clothes, really, but Ryan was desperate to remove them as he tried to push up the shirt and pull her panties down, rushed and careless.

It was not the mood-inducing scene she left moments ago, where Atticus had taken his time with her.

"I'm kind of sleepy," Molly forced out.

"Yeah, well, I'm kind of horny," he shot back in a rough tone.

Molly heard the satiny fabric of her undergarments rip beneath his fingers. Seemed it didn't matter what she wanted, not really. And sadly, to her dismay, it was probably a better idea to simply roll onto her back and let him have his way with her, no matter how not-turned-on she was.

Ryan wasted no time climbing onto her. There was no pre-emptive thought to what she might want. Nothing to get her prepared. He simply leaned down, forced his lips onto Molly's, creating a smacking sound as he sloppily kissed her. He tasted of booze, smelled of stale cigarettes and sweat.

She pinched her eyes closed and tried to envision Atticus, calling him forward, if only to make it easier.

But between the grunts, the kisses, and then the ache caused by his erect penis shoving into her, she was unable to make herself think of something better. She held back the whimper, instead only allowing her chin to quiver as pain flared, and uneasiness wrenched her stomach.

Ryan was quick, at least. And after only a few minutes of thrusting, she could feel him tense above her. He let out a strangled groan, and in the dim light she could see his smile of delight. How could he have enjoyed that? She certainly hadn't, not at all. He was fast and erratic, rough and inconsiderate. There was no intimacy. Just haphazard sex.

He rolled off her, his breathing fast and shallow.

"That was awesome. Just what I needed," he said, and then rolled over. He didn't even take the time to clean himself off, remove his socks, or hold her.

A minute later he was snoring softly.

Tears pricked Molly's eyes. She felt violated. Used. She might have preferred him to leave a hundred bucks on the nightstand and leave, because that's how he'd made her feel. Nothing more than a whore.

She slid from the bed, rushing to the bathroom. Quickly, she climbed into the shower, not caring about temperature. Tears began to stream down her cheeks as she scrubbed her skin raw. She felt dirty, and nothing she could do made that feeling go away. Not really.

Molly didn't usually smoke, but after she toweled off, put on clean pajamas, she slipped one from Ryan's open pack on the kitchen table and went out into the night. She sat on the front stoop of the tiny house she and Ryan shared and lit it. It was silly to think it would calm her nerves, and after a few puffs she put it out and tossed it into the ashtray they kept close by.

"I could kill him!" Atticus appeared to her, pacing the lawn, hands clenched tightly.

Of course, he'd seen everything. He was part of Molly's subconscious.

"No, you couldn't," she said, drawing her knees to her chest, wrapping her arms around, hugging them.

"Yes I could..." He trailed off, coming closer to her. "But you couldn't." He sighed. They were one and the same. Sharing the same mind, body, and soul. And although Atticus, at times, seemed to have all the control, she knew she could never hurt Ryan. She wasn't that person.

"It's okay. Maybe that was enough to get him through the week."

"You shouldn't be treated like that. No one should. Ever."

"Maybe not. But..." She couldn't really make another excuse for him, couldn't actually rationalize what he'd just done.

"But you should leave him. For you. For us. Things could be so much better, I'm sure of it."

If Atticus was saying it, that meant deep down, she had been thinking it. Somewhere. In the deepest darkest reaches of her mind she knew she should leave. Get up, walk down the street and never look back. But what would happen? The tumultuous wrench of uncertainty caused her to get up, heave a sigh, and head back into the life she'd created for herself. Wasn't there a saying? About making beds... She made a choice at one point, and now she felt like she had to live with it.

* * *

Molly didn't write for days. Still unsettled by what Ryan had done. And what Atticus wanted. She couldn't see past the moment. From where she stood, the path to the future seemed bleak. That scared her. Instead of confronting things, she swept them under the invisible rug and chose to believe this was what she truly wanted.

"You can't just push me aside. I'm inside you," Atticus verbalized within her mind.

She'd been shelving books at the library where she worked, when the familiar warmth she felt whenever he was there, spread over her.

"See what I mean? I'm always here, whether you want me or not."

Ignoring the voice, she pushed the cart forward, plucked books from it and deposited them on the shelf. Molly could easily admit she'd missed him. That was the first time they really spent apart since he'd come to her. And Molly hated the yearning in her heart that tugged at the sound of his silky voice.

"Come with me on another adventure, Molly," he said in a singsong voice. "Let me take care of you."

Molly scoffed at the thought. *Take care of her.* That should have been Ryan's job. But since the other night, he'd been even less present. Working later, coming home at all hours of the night. Completely unreliable. Molly wanted to believe it was because he felt sorry about what he'd done, but then, he hadn't yet uttered a word about it. No apology. No declarations of love. In fact, he hadn't shown her any attention whatsoever. There was a lack of morning pecks on the cheek, and after work hugs. It was as though he had checked out of the relationship and was waiting for Molly to catch up. He might have been pushing her away, but Molly, for whatever reason, clung to him.

"We could go to a symphony. Or on a road trip. Or to Paris, I've heard it's nice this time of year."

Molly couldn't help but smile. All of those things, of course, were dreams of hers. And Atticus had always done what he could to make them come true. Even it were only fiction, and they didn't really take a cross-continental flight, time with Atticus felt as good as the real thing.

"I wish I could hold you," Molly whispered.

"You can. Just close your eyes. Imagine my arms wrapped tightly around you. Feel the heat radiating from my skin, warming you."

She did as Atticus said, right there, in the middle of the stacks of books.

Inhaling, she created the illusion. She embraced it. Molly felt Atticus. He tickled her stomach with butterflies; shivered her spine with electricity as it branched out farther, moving from her back to her toes, reaching out to the tips of her fingers. This was the caress of complete consumption. Atticus was everywhere. He was not just in her head, but her heart. He was the reason she got up in the morning and the reason she went to bed at night—the driving force that allowed her to get through the day. She marveled at the sensation and knew it beat out a real hug from anyone, any day.

"Thank you," she exhaled, letting the moment begin to fade away.

"Tonight?"

Molly gave in. "Tonight."

Eager to finish work and escape, Molly began to daydream—with Atticus' help, of course—about what their latest adventure would hold. The story began to take shape. The plot forming like tiny threads weaving together, until, eventually, the need to release it onto the page became so insistent it began to hurt. Aching her body, begging to be liberated.

Ryan wasn't home from work when Molly arrived. She grabbed a couple of snacks from the cupboard, a bottle of water from the fridge, and disappeared into her bedroom, vanishing all-too-quickly into a fairy-tale.

Atticus clutched her hand as they rushed up the steps of the opera house. Her green dress, accented with gold embellishments, billowed around her. Molly tripped on her heel, but Atticus was there to keep her steady. He always was. And when she gave him an encouraging nod, he pulled her the rest of the way up. They were late. Impossibly. But it didn't matter. Atticus was a man of privilege. A hand in all things. He merely flashed an usher, blocking a door, with a smile, and then it was being pushed open.

The music, a melodramatic wail of instruments, swam around Molly. It entered her ears as Atticus pulled her towards a private balcony.

But it was not something one needed to see. Or hear.

It was something meant to be felt.

The way the notes of the piano prickled her skin as each key was pushed. How the cry of violins, the bow being slid over the strings, caused her to quiver. The drums felt as though they thumped in time with her heart pounding against her chest. She felt a breath of air across her face as clarinets and flutes joined the movement. Like the howl of wind on a blustery day...

She wanted to cry for the composer. Believed she knew what they must have been feeling. It was of loss. It circled around her with such reverence, she thought she'd never experience anything purer in her life. It was honest and dramatic, bringing tears to her eyes.

Atticus fingered away the wetness from Molly's cheek. "Are you sad?"

Unsure of how to respond, Molly shook her head. She continued to let the vibrations of the instruments soothe her as one theme began to fade into another. But Atticus was there, taking her hand gently into his. He gave it a heartening squeeze, spending more time watching her and her reactions, than he did the frantic movements of the musicians as they performed with their instruments.

It wasn't all melancholy. Not in the least. Molly sat up straighter when a jubilant theme took over. The joy that swelled inside her was evident as she smiled, her eyes growing wide. Her body gently swayed back and forth, feeling the upbeat melody. Just like life, the composition changed dramatically with each passing note, breaking way for an entirely new reaction to stimulate Molly. She experienced them all: cheerfulness, sympathy, fear, ecstasy. Each one entered Molly and clenched her heart.

When an especially amorous piece began, Atticus leaned in towards her. "Would you dance with me?"

Molly looked around. They were hidden, high up, and away from the masses. There was no one to see and no reason to censor their behavior. She bit her lip and looked up into hazel eyes. He was already standing, his hand out, offering it to her. Molly let her hand skim over his fingers before she hauled herself to her feet, stepping away from her chair.

All at once, Atticus was there. He urged Molly closer, silently commanding her to press against him as he slid his hand over her bare back, down to the small where he held steady. Slowly he began to move. Tiny steps back and forth, guiding Molly to match his actions. Her eyes fluttered closed, letting the music, and Atticus, wash over her. Gently, he pressed his lips to her temple, lingering. Then he held her hand up and rested it against his heart, holding it there. The pulse beneath, entrancing.

Molly shocked herself out of the story, desperate for air. She swallowed thickly, chest heaving, as beads of sweat glistened on her skin. She was overwhelmed by the moment but wasn't ready to let go of it. Molly was desperate for more. Typing with a ferocious burn, Molly evolved the story. It might have been her and Atticus' most alluring scene yet, and she hungered to increase the intensity of it. She wanted it all.

The evening had played out, becoming everything Molly ever wanted. The symphony was on her "most desired" list, and Atticus had delivered it to her. But there was more Molly wanted from him. From the night. Molly wanted to be loved.

As Atticus pushed opened the door to the hotel room they'd stay in, she was eager. Her feet stung from the heels she'd worn and she was quick to kick them from her feet. Atticus undid the tiny clasp that held his bowtie in place, pulling it free. He then unbuttoned his collar, freeing his shirt from his black pants.

He'd presented Molly with his jacket when they took to the streets, walking in the starry night. It had been brisk, and Molly shivered, not just from the cold, but from the music that still pulsed through her. Now, it fell from her shoulders, was folded neatly and slung over the back of a chair.

She stood in the middle of the grand space, larger than any apartment or house she'd ever lived in. Decorated with paintings, striking rugs, and ornate furniture, it was a look fit for a castle. And Molly felt like a princess.

"Come here," he said.

At his strong and commanding tone, Molly melted a little. She moved slowly towards him, closing the distance. She expected him to say something else. When she was within reach, he took her into his arms, encompassing her. Atticus held Molly close, breathed her in, gazing into her eyes. Molly reached up, putting her palm to his cheek, but didn't hold it there for long. She let her fingers dance down his face, his neck, and then to the buttons on his shirt. Unsteadily, she worked her way down the length, revealing his chest. Molly placed her hand to where he had put it earlier, over his heart. The beats were erratic, allowing her to feel a hint of what she was doing to him. How she excited him.

"Kiss me," she breathed, giving him a command of her own.

Atticus was all-too-willing to oblige. He wasted no time pressing his lips against hers. It was soft and supple at first, but became firmer, persistent. He took her bottom lip and nibbled at it, sucking with a tender motion. For Molly, it didn't last long enough as he pulled back to slide his arms from around her neck and down her back. Tenderly, he gave her bottom a little squeeze, pulling her against his stiffness. Like the beat of his heart, the feel of his erection was proof of how undone he was becoming.

She stepped a tiny foot back and reached down, feeling Atticus further. Her hand began to stroke him. Catching him off guard, she boldly dropped her hand into his pants and palmed him. Atticus cleared his throat with a hoarse groan.

"Wait," Atticus said, stilling her hand.

Molly was confused. She wanted to do this for him, to satisfy him. Only, he wouldn't let her. He pulled her hand free and gripped it tightly. Her frown was evident as he leaned in and took it away with another kiss.

"I want to worship you. To decorate your entire body with my kisses. To trace every one of your curves with my hands. To..."

"Yes," Molly moaned. *Take me*, she wanted to say, but couldn't. She was affected so strongly by his words, she had managed all she could say. Anything else that might have passed through her lips would be indecipherable.

Atticus helped Molly free of the confines of her dress. Though it was exquisite, she was thankful to be released from the yards of fabric that stood between them. She meant to help him remove the rest of his suit, but whenever she offered a helping hand, Atticus batted it away with an earnest smile.

When they were bare to each other, Atticus guided her to the bed. He laid her down on her back and proceeded to do as he'd promised, sensually peppering her skin with kisses, rubbing his hands over every inch of exposed skin. He teased her pert nipples with his fingers, only to swirl his tongue around their firmness. Gently he pulled them into his mouth, one at a time, sucking and nibbling. Molly gripped the sheets, fisted them as the sensation warmed her core. And when Atticus' fingers slipped down to her most delicate area, she was wet, lusting after him.

She wheezed, impulsively, as his warm fingers circled her clit and slid inside. Arching her back, she forced herself closer, deepening the movements he made. Atticus teased and pleasured her. He caught her breast in his hand, pinching her nipple slightly, heightening her senses, pushing her closer to the edge.

But he didn't let her fall. Not right away. He made her wait. Atticus seized her in another embrace, forcing her legs around his torso. He was deliberate in his actions as he lingered, then gradually pushed himself inside her. Leisurely at first, relishing the moment as she trembled beneath him. Each inch of him caused another deeper reaction, until he felt her clench around him completely, his erection buried inside of her. Atticus waited until he was certain she was ready for more before moving his hips, increasing his speed.

Molly was unhinged, and she felt the buildup of pressure aching between her legs. It was almost unbearable but was the most enchanting sensation. It clouded her vision. Dizzying her head. And she pinched her eyes shut, readying herself for the ultimate release. She moaned a little louder as her entire body became rigid and firm. She fisted the sheets into her hands tighter and was brought to orgasm. At the last second, Molly's eyes sprung open. She wanted to see him. To see his face when he saw and felt all the effects he had on her. She wasn't the only one consumed by their passion...

* * *

Molly came out of the scene buzzing with electricity. Her entire body felt alive, hot blood racing through her veins. She smiled wide at what she and Atticus had written. It was everything she could have wanted and more. She had been brought to the brink, pushed over the edge, and devoured in all the ways a woman should be. But at that moment, she felt a pang of sadness.

She knew it wasn't real. And that killed her. She hadn't actually made love to Atticus. Not really. For the first time, she realized what she could never truly have with him.

"You can have it, Molly. All of it. You just have to make a choice."

For once, she cursed the fact that Atticus was always there, swimming in her thoughts, injecting himself into the forefront of her brain.

"What choice?"

But, of course, she knew what he was going to say before he had a chance to utter the words.

"No. No I won't choose." Molly frowned. "I don't want to. Don't make me choose."

The whisper of Atticus was loud, as though he were truly standing in the room with her. "You can't have it all, Molly. You can't spend your time with me, but waste your life with him. It's not fair to you, and I can't—"

"Yes, you can, Atticus. You can stay. You can be with me. I need you."

"No. You need the idea of me, to believe that I'm real. But, Molly, I'm not."

Her eyes welled with tears, but she fought against shedding them.

"It's either him or me, Molly. I can't keep being the diversion you use to escape. Not when I want you all to myself."

Molly was conflicted by what he was saying. She had thought their written exploits were enough. That she could spend time with one foot on either side of the real and the truly unreal.

"Think about it, Molly. For me..." His voice began to fade.

"No, wait! Don't go!" she cried.

She heard the rumble of his laughter. "I may disappear, but I am never truly gone. Not unless you release me."

"Atticus!" she yelled, her voice echoing through the empty room. He wasn't going to answer. For now, he was tucked away, waiting in the shadows for when she'd either made up her mind or let go of him completely. Neither choice, to Molly, seemed like the right one.

She took the time to reread what she had written, re-living the perfect moments she and Atticus had together until her heart ached.

Molly then closed the laptop, sliding it under her bed, hidden away. She slept restlessly, hoping Atticus would come to her like he sometimes did, in her dreams. He never did. And she felt Ryan stumble to bed, thankful that he didn't disturb her. Molly didn't think she could put on a brave face for him. She felt broken into pieces and wasn't sure how she'd manage to bring them back together.

* * *

Two days later, Molly sat at the kitchen table, watching Ryan shovel soggy cereal into his mouth. She hadn't been the same since that night, and contemplated what she planned to do. She had fallen in love with the idea of the perfect man.

"Why do you love me?"

Ryan looked up from his meal. He scratched his head. "What do you mean?"

"It's a simple question. Why do you love me?"

Molly couldn't remember why she loved Ryan, or what had brought them together. It had been so long, the past vague and unclear, overshadowed by a million emotions that took precedence.

"Well, you look good naked." He laughed. "And you're a good cook. You take care of me. And put up with my shit."

"Right. Okay. That's good. Anything else?" Molly was saddened by his answers so far.

"What's this about?"

It was probably a good thing he hadn't been drinking, or the conversation might have taken a dramatic turn. But for now, Ryan was calm.

"I just... I'm not sure I'm... Doesn't it feel like something's missing?" *Like your attentiveness,* she thought, but didn't dare say it.

"Um. I'm not sure." Ryan looked at the clock. "I need to head to work."

But she didn't feel like the conversation was over. "Call in sick. Stay with me. Let's spend the day together."

He might have thought about it—for a second, maybe—but to her disappointment, he said, "Is this about flowers?"

"What?"

"Flowers, do you want them? Are you trying to tell me something?"

She shook her head. "No. This isn't about flowers. Nevermind."

Ryan stood from the table, leaned in and kissed Molly on the cheek. She was still staring at the empty chair five minutes later. He couldn't even tell her, for real, why he loved her. The words that should have been easy hadn't come. It created a hole in her heart, a void, because it pushed her one step closer to realizing something. She couldn't imagine spending the rest of her life with someone who couldn't even use any number of descriptive words to prove to her he cared. Not one.

* * *

Molly went more than a week without materializing Atticus. She hadn't made up her mind about her future. Fear of being alone held her firmly in place. She wasn't sure if she had the courage to pack her bags, even if she wanted to. Molly also didn't know if she would ever be content with a life of having Atticus only inside her or written in the stories they created. Certain that would never be enough. And to her, when she thought about it, that was her still ending up alone.

Instead, she poured her attention into her work. It was the only thing, other than Atticus, she loved. There was something enchanting about working in a library, the answers to the world's questions at your fingertips. All that knowledge eager to be soaked up. She often spent her free time flipping through the pages, feeling the old musty bindings, inhaling their archaic prose.

She had the entire library mapped out, memorized. Molly could close her eyes and help just about anyone find just about any book. She also was eager to peruse the catalogs they got in the mail, deciding what new novels, or works of nonfiction, should be added to their ever-growing collection.

"Molly?"

Setting down the book she was holding, Molly turned to see one of the other librarians standing next to a tall, handsome man.

Her heart stopped.

Though not exactly, his features were similar to Atticus'. It was as though he was there, standing in front of her, having aged a few years since the last time she saw him. Blinking rapidly, she tried and failed to make the figment disappear. She wondered if she'd had a few too many cups of coffee, or accidentally taken one of the pills that Ryan sometimes used to get high when things were particularly bad for him.

"Molly?"

She shook her head and looked from the librarian to the man. He was still there. Molly resisted the urge to reach out and touch him.

"Yeah. Sorry. Day dreaming." *And having a heart attack*, she thought.

"Can you help this gentleman? He's looking for 'A Dream within a Dream'."

How ironic, she thought with a laugh. "Yeah. Of course."

"You're in good hands. Molly is the best. I'm sorry I couldn't help. My expertise is more geared towards romance." The librarian swept her eyes over the length of the man seductively and blushed a little when she caught Molly noticing her appraisal of him.

"Thank you, ma'am," the man said, and then turned his attention towards Molly. "So, I'm in good hands?"

"The best. I promise. Why don't you follow me?"

Molly stepped from her cart of books and began to head down one of the towering aisles. She maneuvered her way through the stacks, occasionally looking back just to make sure the man was still there. Still real.

A few seconds later, Molly stopped deep in the back of the library. The poetry section often went unnoticed. Most of the patrons settled on best sellers of fiction rather than something written by someone long since dead. Molly enjoyed reading it though, and she was very familiar with the author of the particular poem she was enlisted to find.

Her fingers dragged across the worn bindings until she plucked a heavy book from the shelf and held it out to the man.

"You have it. The complete works." He looked at the book and then at Molly, amazement in his eyes, as he took it from her. When his hand brushed against hers, it was as though an ember inside Molly had sparked, smoldering.

"It's a great read if you have the patience."

He smiled at her. "No, it's an incredible read. So serious and dark. I've lost my copy somehow. The bookstore in town didn't have it in stock."

"Well, if you sign up for a library card, it can be all yours, for a week."

This caused him to laugh. "That's it? Only a week? Preposterous! Who do I talk to get an extension?"

Molly laughed, the feeling almost odd as it spread over her, that ember, beginning to flame. "I don't think we offer those. You have to come back and check it out again."

"Well, rest assured, Molly, I will be back. Plenty of times, then. It will take me a few weeks, at least, to get through this again. I trust you'll be around, in case I need help finding anything else?"

Molly nodded, biting her lip. "Yeah. Of course, I will be."

"Excellent. Well, I'll let you get back to work."

Without another word, the man took the collected works of Edgar Allan Poe and disappeared into the labyrinth of dusty books and best sellers. Molly rushed to the end of the aisle, just to grab one more look. Just to make sure he was still real. But he was gone.

She pressed her back against a shelf, hand over her heart as she breathed in deeply, counting backward in her head, eyes pinched tightly closed. She had an entirely new feeling flaring inside her. It swallowed a bit of the uncertainty she always felt. It absorbed a bit of the lacking self-esteem that often held her back, because she was pretty sure he had flirted with her. It had been a while. A long while. But she was positive she could recognize the gesture. For the first time in forever, especially since Atticus left, there was hope, no matter how small the glimmer of it was.

Lighter on her feet, Molly all but skipped through the door of her house. The gray cloud that had settled over her had begun to lift, or so she thought. The living room was turned upside down. Couch toppled over, books strewn across the floor and the small coffee table broken in two. Molly's heart began to race, for an entirely different reason than it had before, as she edged further into the chaotic mess.

The kitchen was in disarray. Cupboards open, contents were strewn about. Dishes shattered against the wooden floor. On the table, a bouquet of flowers rested, an unusual sight. Molly had begun to pull out her cell, to call the police to report a robbery, when she heard footsteps coming down the hallway.

Ryan came into view and she could tell, without a doubt that he had been drinking. His features turned harsh when he saw her. Only, he hadn't come alone.

Cradled in his arms were her computer and the countless notebooks she had hidden under her bed, filled with her and Atticus' many trysts.

"Where-where did you get those?" She admitted the hiding spot wasn't creative. But Ryan never had a need to look under the bed. Ever. He didn't pick up his clothes from the floor, or sweep the dust bunnies from the corners. He'd never once picked up a rag to help her clean on a Saturday morning when she wore her hair in a ponytail and scrubbed their house from top to bottom. He'd spent that time in his recliner, a beer in his hand, and the TV blaring.

"Does it matter?"

It didn't. Not really. She already knew the answer.

He walked past her and dumped the load onto the table. She turned, just in time to see him sweep his arm over the surface and send her romance to the floor. The laptop fell with a crunch. He stomped on the books with his boot covered heel.

"What the fuck, Molly?" he yelled at her. She stepped back at the loudness, shying away from his angered voice. "What the fuck is all this?"

"Stories. That's it. Nothing more." She instinctively took another step back.

"Sure the hell doesn't read like nothing."

Because they weren't. They were dreams within a dream. They were all the things she still wanted to do with her life. The places she wanted to go. The love she desired. They were her heart and soul, poured out onto the pages. Her blood, sweat, and tears, mixed with what she knew—if only a little—she deserved and what she could've gotten out of life, if only she could have been stronger.

He closed the distance, seizing her arms, gripping them so tightly it hurt. It scared her.

"Are you having an affair?" he spat in her face.

"No. I swear, I—"

Ryan pushed her back, just as he let the ironclad grip he had on her go. She fell fast and hard.

"I don't fucking believe you!" He knelt to the ground, grabbing at her again. "After all I've done for you. I've taken care of you, and this, *this* is how you repay me, you slut." He raised his hand as if to strike her. She braced for it.

The searing white hotness that flared violently over her cheek caused fireworks to shoot behind her eyes.

She cried out and scrambled to get away, worried he would hit her again.

From out of nowhere, Molly screamed. "Atticus!" She yelled it again. But as Ryan looked around the kitchen, unsure if someone would come to Molly's aide, she realized something. *Help would never come.* Not for her. The one person she cared most about in the world wasn't real. Atticus couldn't save her, just like he couldn't ever really be there for her. He couldn't offer her a life. Not the one she wanted. Tears welled in her eyes. It occurred to her, for the first time, just how imaginary he was. *He wasn't real.* Not even close. Sure, he may have offered her a life, but at what cost? Her sanity?

Her muse. The creative spirit inside her soul had become one of her greatest conflicts. She had spent so much of the last few months wrapped up in the need to feel loved, that she found it in the entirely wrong place. Atticus had enabled her. He hadn't let her see life exactly how it was. The lines between reality and fantasy had become so blurred that Molly had lost her way.

She had wanted to create stories. To not feel alone. But what she really needed was to stand on her own two feet. To understand she could have everything she wanted if she would just simply reach out and take it, knowing for sure she was deserving.

Ryan and Atticus had power over her only because she allowed it. But not anymore. She had seen someone, a stranger, pay just that bit of extra attention towards her. Which meant she was worthy of affection. It didn't have to come from a drunken boyfriend or an imaginary muse. It could come from anywhere. She just had to open her eyes. That feeling had sparked the ember, causing the flame, but now it was up to her to stoke the fire and let it rage.

Molly pushed herself from the floor, standing unsteadily. "I deserve better. Better than you," she spoke slowly, clearly, assuredly. She turned and headed out of the kitchen. To her surprise, Ryan let her go. Molly hesitated at the door. She looked back to see Ryan looking confused, but she also saw the collection of her and Atticus on the floor. Instead of caring, she turned and walked away. She didn't need them, either of them, anymore.

"That's it, that's your choice?"

Molly didn't bother replying to the voice of Atticus inside her head. He already had his answer, because he had been a part of her.

Atticus might have shown her love and affection. He allowed her to dream, to create, and as it turned out, to prepare her for the future. He had also showed her how to be strong; what real love should be like when she finally found someone to open her heart to.

As Molly walked down the street, arms wrapped around herself, having left everything behind, she smiled. She wondered if she had created Atticus based on someone she had seen once, no matter how briefly. And that deep down, maybe she had always known her perfect man, the character in her forever story, was really out there, but she just wasn't ready to see that.

Until now.

Filling in the Blanks

LILAH BURST through the doors, breathless. She was late and thankful when no one seemed to raise their eyes towards her. She might not have been able to handle that; blushing fiercely, tripping over her own feet, and creating even more of a scene. Instead, she was able to work her way through the seated crowd and find an open chair at the back of the auditorium.

She settled in her seat, pulled out her notebook, and tried catch up with what was being said. By the program she had read earlier, Lilah remembered that this was a panel about genres and subgenres, and the next big thing. A mash-up of conversation, really, because reading was subjective. What one person loved, the next would hate. And judging the market was nearly impossible when it came to which genres sell and which ones didn't. There was no true way to know what would inspire readers and send them to the bookstores. It was always a big gamble.

"Who are you with?"

Turning, Lilah settled her eyes on the person beside her. He was young, maybe about sixteen, hair curling over his ears and in his eyes. He pushed it aside and smiled at her. Funny, she'd been sure the seat had been empty just a minute ago. But then, she hadn't been paying that much attention as she quickly plunked down and began to listen, immersed in what the panel of industry professionals had been saying.

"Me?" she answered back, confused.

"Yeah, who are you here with?" he repeated as he tapped a pencil on his own pad of paper, a few messy scrawls visible.

Lilah was still uncertain what he meant. "Myself, I guess. I mean, I'm just taking notes."

He laughed. "You must have come with someone, or are you a newbie?"

The statement felt odd as it washed over her. Why couldn't she have come by herself? There was nothing wrong with that, was there?

"Well, I am. Here. By myself," she said defensively and decided to stand from her seat. She made her way to the end of the makeshift aisle and tiptoed across the worn brown carpet, closer to the front, eyes narrowed on another empty seat. There were two together, and she jumped at the chance to move closer, still intrigued by what the panel was about. The attendees around her, who seemed to be listening, engrossed, still hadn't even bothered to acknowledge her presence as she shoved her way through another aisle stepping on toes, kicking over a purse, and nearly falling into an open lap.

When she had made it to her new seat, she adjusted her top, smoothed down her pants and sat with a sigh of relief. She uncapped her pen, poised to take notes.

"Werewolves have been played out. No one's buying them," one of the panelists said. But another was quick to toss out, "True. Publishers aren't. But readers still are."

"And dystopian, if you haven't already written one, sold it and it's in the queue to get published, it ain't worth a damn anymore," another one said.

Lilah wrote down what had been said and adjusted in her seat, leaning forward slightly, just to make sure that she heard everything clearly.

"Mermaids are just breaking the market, now, but again, don't bother writing one. You have to remember, that what is coming out tomorrow was written years earlier. You're actually trying to figure out what readers want four years from now, and not what they want to read in a week."

That made sense to Lilah and she scribbled feverishly.

"But there are some things that never grow tiresome."

"Like vampires?" Someone from the audience shouted out.

"As long as they don't sparkle," the panelist, a man, with brown hair and glasses said with a grin. He looked very studious, more so than the others, and Lilah had wondered who he was. "Like I said, Vampires are still attracting readers, but I think there is a fine line that can't be crossed. There can only be one sparkly vampire, human girl, and an unhealthy relationship, out there."

"Horror always sells. It never gets old. There are always new and interesting ways to kill people and readers are drawn to that. Suspense and thrillers, too."

This got the audience to laugh. At the mention of horror, Lilah got a sickening rumble in her tummy. She wrote the word down, only to cross it out, as she noticed she'd done with some of the other genre's and sub-genre's, and basically anything else they'd talked about. She was starting to wonder why she was there. None of it sounded as appealing as she'd hoped.

"I'm with her."

Lilah jumped with a yelp, her body becoming rigid. She craned her head to the left, looking over her shoulder, towards the voice that had caressed the back of her neck, sending the tiny hairs to raise up. It gave her a chill.

His hand was still pointed forward, towards the panelist on the far right. She was older, mid-fifties, maybe, glasses and graying hair. She wore a simple black top and a pink cable knit sweater over it. Very old fashioned.

"What?" she said, annoyed.

"I'm with her. She's brilliant. I've given her tons of ideas about her latest work."

"That's great. Good for you. But if you don't mind..." She left the end of the sentence hanging in the air between them as she turned back around.

"The name's Eric, and you know, I think you're in the wrong place." Eric leaned far forward, resting his arms on the back of the empty chair beside her. He steepled his fingers as he continued, "You look more like some guy's wet dream. I think you've got your genre already figured out."

Did he just say that? To her? Out loud? Self-consciously she looked around, expecting to see angry faces from the disruption. When it appeared no one had heard, Lilah exhaled, and said, "Excuse me?" She shook her head, thinking perhaps it would have been better to just ignore him.

"No, I meant it as a compliment. Sorry. I'm a teenage guy. I see boobs and ass before anything else," he said as though that was a perfectly reasonable explanation.

"Yeah, thanks. Look, I really want to hear this. It's important."

Eric seemed to get the picture and leaned back in his chair, folding his arms over his chest. Lilah sighed, and looked down at herself. Was she some guy's wet dream, as he had put it? Maybe, a little, she thought, not remembering getting dressed in the morning, or if that had been what she was trying for. Her top might have been a little low cut, dipping between her breasts, hugging her curves. The jeans were tight, and though the heels on her feet caused an ache, she liked the way they looked.

As if the panel had heard Eric's comment, one of them said, "Sex sells. It always has. Boundaries are continually being pushed, and these days, you can get away with anything." *When had they jumped to that?* she wondered, letting out a huff, having missed the last few minutes.

The pen in Lilah's hand began to write. Sex. It gave her the opposite feeling of when they had talked about horror, for sure. This gave her a tickle that spread through her insides.

"See? Some guy's wet dream. I'm more of a hardy boy meets... well, I don't remember what, but I've heard her say it a few times before."

Instead of giving Eric the satisfaction of a response, she simply pressed her lips together and shushed him. But she had lost focus, heat radiating inside her. She wiggled in her chair but couldn't seem to make the tantalizing sensation go away.

"Like I said. You're in the wrong place. They're talking about romance in the next room. Maybe that'll spark something more." He flashed her a lopsided grin.

She'd had enough. She turned all the way around in her chair and yelled, "Shut up!"

He laughed at her. Lilah flushed with embarrassment and frustration, chin quivering.

"Okay, okay." He raised his hands like a white flag. "But you're here for a reason. Gaining perspective, perhaps. But just wait. The people around here get kinda crazy. This is my third time, and if you haven't found someone to be with yet, you will."

Whatever he was blabbing on about only infuriated Lilah further. She threw up her arms in protest and stood from her chair. "Thanks. For ruining this for me."

"Anytime, babe."

His cocky grin needed to be slapped off his face, Lilah thought, as she gathered up her paper, pen and her purse. She was halfway down the aisle when he called out to her, "Romance is in the room on the left. It's a riot. All nipples and wet folds."

"God, grow up!" She clamped her hand over her mouth. *Please, please, no one say anything to me*, she thought, as she made it to the end of the aisle and sprinted, as best she could in her heels, towards the door.

"Trust me, I wish I could!"

* * *

The door slammed shut behind her, and she pressed her back against it, breathing heavily. When she felt composed, she pulled out the program from her purse. She flipped through the pages, trying to figure out what to attend next. Most of the panels were an hour long, so she had plenty of time still, to slip into the back of another one.

Nothing of interest jumped out at her, not really. She scanned the titles, read the descriptions and finally settled on one about character-building.

Lilah walked through the hotel, passed by the stairs and headed for the elevator. Impatiently, she waited, and when the doors opened she was nearly toppled over as a girl rushed out, slamming her shoulder into Lilah. She wobbled unsteadily, but was able to keep herself upright.

Rude! The girl hadn't even bothered to stop and apologize. She shook off the encounter and slipped through the closing elevator doors just in time to ride it up.

On the second floor, she read the nameplates on the doors until she found the one she wanted. This time, she slowly turned the knob until she felt it release and gently pulled it open, just wide enough for herself to get through.

This was a much smaller room than the other, and many of the seats were empty. She had her pick, but still chose to slip in and sit at the back. She settled into the plush paisley, pulled out her pen and paper, and again, tried to figure out what was being talked about.

"You need to know who you're writing about. Who your character is. Think about them in terms of a person, a friend, and create a life for them. Give them more than just basic demographics. Think deeper, create a past, if you want."

That seemed like a smart idea. Lilah knew people weren't flat. They had a history. Not just birthdays. So she wrote that down on her page.

"You're really pretty. Do you have one?"

Lilah looked up from her notes to find a girl looking towards her. She smiled warmly and waved her hand. She had red hair, green eyes, and freckles on her cheeks. She had almost expected it to be Eric, but was thankful it wasn't. Lilah returned the friendly gesture with a smile of her own. This stranger had a pleasant face, and she doubted she'd have strange outbursts in the middle of the panel.

"Have one what?"

"A birthday. Sorry," she pointed towards the notebook cradled in Lilah's lap, "I shouldn't have been spying on you like that."

Lilah laughed and waved her hand. "It's okay. And yeah, of course I do. Who doesn't?" she said, not meaning for it to come out the way it did. Sounding absurd. But as the stranger frowned, she felt guilty.

"What it is? I don't know mine. That's why I'm here. Sort of trying to hash out all my details. I'm Cassandra, by the way."

It was a peculiar thing to say, but Lilah didn't give it much thought, not quite being able to figure out what she had meant by it. Cassandra looked a little jittery like she'd had one too many cups of coffee that morning. But when Lilah went to reply, opening her mouth, she couldn't remember what was supposed to come out. It was on the tip of her tongue, she swore, and yet, no matter how much she tried, she couldn't form the words.

"It's okay. You don't have to tell me. I'd guess late twenties or early thirties. It's always hard to tell that about someone. Probably the most difficult thing to come up with. You know, male or female, age, hair color, and eye color. You need all that before you can come up with the rest."

Having just been tongued-tied, it took Lilah a second or two before she found her words again. "Yeah, that's true. That's what actually starts the development process." But couldn't figure out why that shivered her with an unnerving feeling. She'd met some strange people so far, but then, eccentric did often come with the territory.

She made a few more notes on her pad, letting her hand take over, and writing out whatever it wanted to.

"See, there you go." The stranger smiled.

When Lilah looked down at the blue writing, she had written a few things about herself. Or at least, she thought they were about herself. As she read the words back, it became clearer in her mind. She was twenty-nine. That felt right. Born in late January, on the 22nd. She could still tell people she was in her twenties. It made her feel younger, somehow. But then, suddenly, she looked down at her low cut top, skinny jeans and heels, thinking that might not be the best outfit to be running around in. She'd have to remember to change it later.

"Yeah, thanks. It's hard stuff."

"Just wait till you have to decide the other details. I mean, are you single, married, in a committed relationship? What's your plot going to be about, what do you do for a living, where do you live?"

Thinking about it, Lilah came up empty. Even stranger, she thought, as she closed her eyes, to realize she couldn't quite remember who she was. It had been there a second ago, hadn't it?

"Don't listen to her."

Another voice joined the conversation, as Lilah began to feel a little dizzy and lightheaded. When she opened her eyes again, another friendly face was turned towards her.

"You don't have to know all that right away. There's always the delete button. Nothing's concrete. Nothing in this life is permanent, not until your story is bound in a book if you're lucky enough to get that far."

Cassandra was quick to add, "You're thinking too hard. It's not going to all fall into place at once." Then she added, with concern, "Maybe put your head down between your legs. Might make that nasty case of uncertainty go away."

Doing as she'd been told, Lilah stuck her head down, letting her forehead rest on her thighs. Her long brown hair touched the floor and tickled the tops of her feet. Inhaling a few deep breaths helped calm her further.

"Oh, sorry, I didn't know you were a newbie. Now that I'm looking, you are a little green around the edges."

Lilah raised her head. "I am not." She looked at her bare arms. "Am I?" she added as if she'd be tinged with color, and hadn't been able to see it clearly.

"She didn't mean literally," Cassandra said with a laugh. "I've been here for three days, mapping things out. I practically feel like an old timer, but things are still fuzzy."

Relating, with the fuzziness, Lilah nodded. "What about you?" she asked, directing her question to the other girl.

"Oh, I came here with someone. I've got it all mostly figured out. Just making the rounds, trying to get a little more inspiration for a prequel. Figuring out the backstory that hadn't much mattered until my first book was finished."

After that, the three of them settled into a comfortable silence, and by the end of the panel, Lilah had made a few more notes in her notebook. But for just as many facts she'd managed to figure out, she had just as many unanswered questions still looming in the air. It had been like she'd woken up with a sense of loss—amnesia maybe—and she was trying to put all the pieces of her story back into place.

"There's a social tonight, in one of the ballrooms. You should come. Might help you figure out a few more things, and maybe you'll be lucky enough to meet someone and make a connection, that's always the best part about these things."

"Sure, yeah. There's a few more panels I want to check out."

Lilah joined in and clapped with the rest of the people around her, having missed the last minutes of the panel. She hadn't minded, this time, losing a bit of her concentration to make new friends.

"Great! Well, I'm out of here. I really do hope to see you there!"

Walking out of the conference room, with Cassandra at her side, Lilah felt a little more comfortable. And when Cassandra leaned in for a hug, Lilah graciously returned it.

"It was nice meeting you!" Lilah said.

"You'll do great. I swear, no one really knows how to go about finding the story. It's a huge learning curve. I showed up practically naked, and look at me now."

Lilah laughed. "You look great."

"Yeah well, thanks, I just need to figure out the rest of what's in here." She tapped her temple with her finger.

"And remember, don't think too hard about it. I've found the best way to figure it all out is to just listen, close your eyes, and you'll get it."

"Thanks again," Lilah said and waved goodbye to Cassandra. She took a few steps towards the elevator but stopped, and turned around. Cassandra was gone, perhaps swallowed up by the horde of conference attendees that had begun to spill out of the other rooms.

She felt a pang of sadness as she realized she'd have to spend the next while on her own, and could only hope she'd find someone else to talk to at the next panel. She'd been learning just as much from the discussion panels as she had from the new friends she'd met.

* * *

By the end of the day, Lilah had filled three pages with notes. She'd absorbed everything that had been said around her, and began to write out the basics of her plot line. In doing so, she'd started to fill the holes that had been poked through her brain and was starting to see things unfold.

Not only did she know a bit of the back-story she'd been missing, she'd begun to create the future she was hoping for. She'd settled on a genre. Eric, from the morning, had been right. She was all about steamy romance. Attending a panel about romantic firsts and how to make them realistic sent shivers up her spine and teased her with sensation. There was something about sensual kisses and feather-light touches that curled her toes. She had confirmed that further when she slipped into the wrong panel—one about fantasy creatures—and was weirded out when they talked about dragons and trolls. And she certainly wasn't into witches or vampires, whether they sparkled or not, no matter how alluring that might have seemed. The taste of blood hadn't sounded all that appetizing—gross, really—and she wasn't about to join in any spell castings or séances. They had been a bizarre bunch, and it turned her off of the idea of anything fantastical, or anything that went bump in the night. She was more of a contemporary girl, so far.

Lilah had discovered the intricacies of dialogue and how important it was. It painted a picture, because once she knew about all the different kinds of dialects and techniques, her impending narrative discovered a location, a time period, and more. Cassandra had been right, it was better to take things slow. When she pushed herself too hard, thinking about all the components and sequences of events that made up a novel, she had begun to suffer from vertigo, the room spinning, her head growing fuzzy. Too much, too soon, and she had to understand that great fiction took time to initiate.

Feeling almost whole, Lilah entered the party, a room brightly lit from chandeliers of drop crystals that hung from the ceilings. The twinkle of rainbows cast on the tables adorned with simple black table cloths, and the matte colored walls.

She looked around nervously, feeling a little out of place as she stood awkwardly in the entryway, her notebook pressed firmly again her chest. But then, Lilah saw a fiery red head, with freckles dappled over her cheeks, bouncing through the crowd towards her. Cassandra.

Relaxing only slightly, Lilah smiled and waved at the welcoming face quickly closing the distance between them.

"I'm glad you came!"

Lilah replied, unsure of herself, "Thanks, though I'm not sure this was a good idea."

Cassandra was quick to shoot back, "Of course it is! This is where all the magic happens."

"The what?" She raised an eyebrow to further show her confusion. Cassandra wasn't serious, was she?

Rolling her eyes, Cassandra looped her arm with Lilah, not answering the question, but instead, began to push her way through the crowd, yanking Lilah forward. "Come on, there's more of us to meet," she tossed over her shoulder.

Unsteady on her heels, Lilah tried to keep up, as she moved through the jam-packed ballroom. People were everywhere, huddled over high-top tables, seated at lower ones, leaning up against the lengths of walls. And the chatter— it was so loud it caused an ache behind Lilah's eyes.

A million voices could be heard, swirling in the air. Her senses heightened. A plethora of different aromas stung the inside of her nose, causing it to wrinkle. Her eyes tearing up from the invasion of vibrant colors, the ache in her head increasing to a throb. It was almost too much. Overwhelming. She had never seen so many different people in one place. She began to slow, fighting against Cassandra's hold.

"I don't feel so well," Lilah muttered, barely audible.

Slowing her pace, and then stopping, Cassandra turned to her, gripping Lilah's arms. "I know. Sort kicks you right in the gut doesn't it? You sort of feel like you're being pulled apart, in a dozen different directions, right?"

Once Lilah's eyes were closed, she could agree, that's kind of how it felt, but not quite. The darkness that consumed her was frightening. She couldn't decide what was worse; being over stimulated by the room, churning her, or the never ending vast of nothingness, when she tried to tune it all out.

"You just have to adjust to it. It'll get easier. It's just a lot of people searching for inspiration all at once. And hey, if you're lucky, you won't have to come back tomorrow."

At the delightful thought, Lilah opened her eyes. She could get through it. Besides, they were all there for the same reason, right? They all had something in common. They were readers, and writers, they were searching for that next big idea, desperate for a discovery, something that would get those creative juices flowing. Lilah hadn't filled up entire pages of her notebook in hopes of not latching on to a bright idea.

"Hey, there's my wet dream from this morning."

Of course, Eric would be here, Lilah thought, when she and Cassandra had begun to advance forward again. He held a drink in his hand and raised it towards her with that arrogant tease in his tone.

"I see you haven't grown up yet," Lilah said.

"Maybe not. Impossible really, but I see that you have." He let out a whistle. "Seems you managed to make a few revelations about yourself. It's really made you glow."

She might not have liked how he worded things, or the tone he used, but that did make her smile.

"Lilah's a quick learner," Cassandra said proudly. "I bet you she makes a connection, for sure, by the end of the night, and we'll all still be stuck here tomorrow."

"Hey, watch who you're talking to. I've already made a connection," Eric said with mock hurt. "I've got at least three more books before things on my end become obsolete."

"Yeah, well, we can't all be that lucky. There is such a thing as a stand-alone."

Injecting herself into the conversation, Lilah said, "What the hell are you guys talking about?"

Eric and Cassandra laughed. "You really don't know, do you?" Eric said.

"Know what?"

"Oh, babe, you've still got a lot to learn."

That hadn't answered her question, at all. In fact, it raised a few more and as she opened her mouth to reply Cassandra said, "Oh hey, Lilah, I think you've got a looker." Her eyes lit up as she pushed her finger forward, pointing at something Lilah couldn't seem to see. She strained her neck, standing on her tip-toes.

"Oh wait, no, sorry."

And then Lilah saw it, sort of a radiance through the mass of bodies. A boy, who looked much too young to be at a party, was walking toward a woman about Lilah's age. No, that wasn't quite right, he'd almost floated towards her, a smile on his face. And then, though she could have sworn she had imagined it, the boy seemed to dissolve into the air until he was gone. A truly bizarre sight, and she might have wondered if someone had spiked her drink if only she had had one.

"Where'd he go?" The concern in Lilah's voice was evident. "Did you see that?"

Eric said, waving his hand nonchalantly, "Don't worry. He's fine. In a better place, really. He just found the rest of his story, is all."

What did that even mean? Still gaping, she said, "You guys are crazy, you know that." But then, she had begun to wonder if that was true. Maybe she was the one who was crazy...

"Oh, we know. I wouldn't have believed it myself, had I not seen it the other day." Cassandra smiled. "It's kind of cool, too. I can't wait for it to happen to me."

Lilah reached for the glass that was sitting in front of Cassandra. "Did Eric roofie you?" She smelled the contents of the clear bubbly liquid.

"It's just Seven-Up. Do I look old enough to drink?"

Setting the glass back down, Lilah shrugged. "No, I guess not. Doesn't mean he didn't slip something in there. Maybe they are pumping something in through the air ducts, because I swore I just saw a kid fade into thin air. And you two are being totally nonchalant about it."

"Hey, I'm standing right here," Eric said. "I'd appreciate it if you didn't talk about me like I don't exist."

"Well, you don't, not really," said a newcomer to the table. He was a gangly guy, in his twenties, still had pimples on his face, an awkward stance, and a nervous twitch. "The probability of any of us making it to the end of a first draft isn't very high. Do you know how many people start writing a book and never finish it?" When no one answered him, he said, "Neither do I, but it's got to be an enormous number. They don't call it "aspiring" for nothing. Most people just dabble and think it's fun to call themselves a serious writer." He air-quoted the "serious" for emphasis. "But to be an author, well, that's another matter entirely. There's a lot more that goes into it than just words. I mean, there's editing—slicing and dicing a manuscript to shreds, really weeding out the useless prose and characters. And then, what comes next, I mean, even if you do end up with a polished manuscript, nothing says it's publishable. There's a lot of crap out there that gets written, only to collect dust on a shelf somewhere, or be locked in a computer."

Lilah looked at Eric and Cassandra. Their expressions likely matched hers, wide eyed and slack jawed.

Eric punched the guy in the arm. "Way to bring down the party."

Cassandra looked as though she had a twinkle in her eyes, star struck. "You-you sure know a lot." She blushed, making her freckles stand out even more.

"Yeah, well, I've been around for a while. The knowledge I have trapped inside, it's a little scary, and I've yet to find my home."

"Gee, I can't imagine why." Eric let out a huff of air. Then he reached for Lilah's notebook, snatching it out of her hand.

"Hey! That's personal. Give it back." She lunged, but he stepped back just out of her reach. He raised the notebook up in the air. She may have been older, but he was most definitely taller.

"Oh, come on, just let me have a peek."

"No way." She jumped up and tried to reach it for it. She looked to Cassandra for help, only she was engrossed in a conversation with the slightly nerdy newcomer. But it was already too late, Eric had flipped the cover open. "Please, don't." She gave up and covered her face with her hands.

"I knew it!" He snapped his fingers.

Cassandra had chosen that moment to look up. "Knew what?"

"She's all about the romance. Wants to be swept off her feet. Oh, and there's some naughty stuff in here. This is totally not PG. Perhaps, I'm in the wrong storyline." He winked at her.

"Most girls want that. You'd be wise to pay attention. The average writer includes some element of a love interest."

Cassandra beamed at the new addition to the table. "I'm more of a coming of age. But you really think that?"

"Oh sure."

Cassandra giggled, blushing crimson again.

"Yeah, well, I've got a spank bank that tells me I don't need that romance crap," Eric was quick to toss in.

Lilah was mortified. "You're disgusting." Then she held out her hand. "Give it back, now," she demanded, raising her voice a little.

"Alright. Fine. But a waitress? Really. That's the best you could come up with? Why not shoot for the stars and go straight for call girl? Might get you that action you're craving a little quicker."

Cassandra had a blank expression, and the new-comer had bits of drool at the corners of his lips as he gave Lilah more of a once-over with his eyes.

"Just forget about it." Lilah heaved a sigh. She didn't need the notebook, not really. She was pretty confident in who she'd become and what the elements of her story would include. "Cassandra, I think I'm just going to go get some fresh air." She then turned to the guy that had captured her friend's interest. "It was nice meeting you..."

"Oh, yeah, sorry, socially inept." He rubbed his hand over his cord pants and then held it out towards Lilah. She took it. "I'm Bryan."

"Well, it was nice to meet you. You might want to get Cassandra, here, away from this douchebag."

Cassandra and Bryan laughed, and Lilah could see the sparks flying between them, maybe more so once she left the picture.

"I could come with you, you know, if you want," Cassandra said, but her expression, the longing look in her eyes told Lilah she'd only said that to be polite.

"No, I'm good. You have fun." She winked.

Not bothering to retrieve her notebook or say goodbye to Eric, Lilah stepped back from the table and took a few steps towards the entrance.

But all too quickly, she felt a shudder. Goosebumps prickled her skin, and she suddenly felt as though she was being pulled in a different direction. Hesitantly, she looked over her shoulder and found Cassandra with her eyes.

"Yes! I win. I knew it!" She bounced happily.

"You knew what?" Lilah asked, but an extraordinary feeling took hold of her. Instead of waiting for an answer, something inside told her to look back around, in the direction she had been about to go.

It was as though the mass of people parted as she began to walk forward, her attention suddenly drawn to something at the other end of the room.

"Just go with it. It's a good thing."

She heard Cassandra call after her, as a man, standing tall, wearing jeans and a t-shirt came into view. He was all she could see, everything around her washing away. The sound of the voices became muted. She no longer noticed the animated colors of the room that had created a headache earlier. The loss that had consumed her at the start of the day was no longer there, instead making way for even more ideas to come flooding in. She couldn't make sense of what was happening, and she found herself yanking against the invisible reel, fighting against the pull.

"No, don't do that. Go. Tell him about your story. What you want to be written." Cassandra's voice, barely a whisper, managed to reach Lilah's ears, calming her.

Despite the urge to fight it, Lilah let herself be drawn towards the man, her eyes fluttering closed as images began to fill her brain. She started to see things more clearly, the rest of the story, the plot holes that she couldn't have worked out on her on. When she re-opened them, she'd moved more than fifty feet in a fraction of a second, almost floating on the current that had somehow connected her with him.

And then, all at once, she felt overcome with joy. She could have sworn that his gray eyes were lit up with an emotion Lilah couldn't have even begun to describe. But it made her tingle—a zip of electricity that jolted her awake—because this was where she was always meant to be. She wanted to reach out and wrap her arms around him like he was her other half and she wasn't complete without him. She was anxious to feel consumed, and discovering what that meant for her.

Lilah did reach for him. When the final bits of distance were closed, she reached out with her hands and placed them on his chest just as a blazing white light flashed behind her eyes. She felt dizzy, and then, abruptly, before she could have stopped it, she felt herself falling into the abyss. Had she been able to scream, she might have, but fear of the unknown was the last thing she thought, wondering what would happen to her next. And then, that too faded away until she was gone.

* * *

Ethan Young woke up with the inexplicable urge to write, something he hadn't felt in a good long while. The dreams he had the night before created an image in his mind and began to weave together the plot of a novel idea.

Rubbing his hands over his face, he wiped away the sleep from his eyes. He had thought he might lay there for a few more minutes absorbing and marveling at the new outline. Only he didn't want it to slip through his grasp like so many had before.

He rose from the bed, slipped on some boxers and sat at his computer, having been left idle if such an occasion had arisen. He needed to always be at the ready, waiting, utilizing his surrounding, in hopes of gaining back what he had begun to think was infinitely lost.

It had been more than months since putting fingers to the keyboard, and having the inclination to type words, being able to produce something he might have been proud of. He had started many things but could never work through the intricate web of plots and characters in order to finish. Always floundering or losing the nerve to write. It might have been the lack of sales of his previous novel, or the dissolution of his relationship, or... hell, he had lost his muse, the creative ember in his soul that occasionally sparked and flared, burning just a little bit brighter, whispering in his ear.

But he could hear it now. That whisper, beckoning for him to press the keys; it had a story it wanted to be written. He could close his eyes and envision it all laid out before him. Normally, he might have been considered a plotter, taking his time, making notes, and starting something fresh only when he had most of the bones, the skeleton of the novel, outlined. He would have pondered over his characters until they had begun to feel like friends. Until he knew everything there was to know about them; planning elaborate back-stories, giving them parts of himself like quirks and personal traits, making them unique, and perhaps, overly complex. And he'd scour the internet or magazines until he could see in his mind's eye the scenery that would set the stage; details like month and time of year. He'd know, before setting out, if it was to snow, covering the landscape with a dusting of powder, or if the pavement was scorching hot, the air humid and suffocating. Particulars would have been worked out to the finest detail.

This time, though, he didn't give himself the chance to overwork the proposal that was developing. He clearly could hear, and feel, what it wanted, and so without further thought, only pausing to inhale one last deep breath of air, he allowed the voice to take over.

It had been a warm October day, but within the air you could smell a hint of the impending snow that was soon to come over the horizon.

*The leaves on the trees had turned from lus-
cious and vibrant greens to tinged with oranges
and browns. They hung wary against limbs, as
a breeze circled around their stumps and on
the branches, causing a few more to flutter to
the ground. Kids had begun to rake them up,
jumping into the piles. The thin, crisp foliage
rustled with a scratch that grated on ears but
was overshadowed by laughter. He wrote.*

*A girl, with a natural, unabashed beauty,
hurried down the pavement, her heels clicking
against the concrete sidewalk. Long legs made
way to sensual curves, an hour glass figure ac-
centuated by a few extra pounds she might
have been carrying. But it would go mostly unnoticed to anyone. Because the buttons on her
jacket were tight, straining the fabric against
her well-endowed chest, a part of her she
wished could have been different. It tended to
be what men noticed first, second and third,
perhaps even fourth in comparison to her other
features, concentrating on only that. But her
long mahogany hair swayed against her back
with each step she took. The subtle qualities of
her imperfect skin tone, blemishes of red
cheeks, pale and thin lips, and a nose with a
slight crook in the bridge, may have lacked
slightly in attractiveness. But that had been
made up for by her lustrous blue eyes. The
shade of cornflowers spanning a field in the*

summer sun, glistening with drops of dew. They were large orbs, framed by long eyelashes and manicured eyebrows. That should have always been the first thing that was noticed about her. How they always seemed to be consumed with emotion and desire.

Ethan smiled proudly at what he had typed, but didn't dare stop for fear of losing her. He was worried one misstep would take the entire moment and shatter the perfect image he had just created; a woman that should have been beautiful, that was beautiful to him. She may have lacked self-esteem and wore her timidity out in the open. But there was something missing. Eventually, when he was over a dozen pages in, it clicked, and he knew what it was.

As she worked, cleaning the counters, wiping down the espresso machine and mopping the floors, a gentle lullaby could be heard passing through her lips. She hummed a tune, added words, letting the inner music she heard become her soundtrack. It made the time pass, and today, her day-off, needed a little extra to get her through another long shift. The idea of a few more hours and extra tips was something she couldn't turn down; having an eye on a set of new watercolours at the local art store. Not to mention, she was reliable. She couldn't say no. No matter how much she would have liked to stay curled up in a down-filled blanket, a book in her hand, or sitting at her easel with paint in her hair...

Finally, it was closing time, and she was sure she'd never felt more exhausted in her life. The flow of constant customers never really seemed to die down, everyone rushing into the cafe for a cup of coffee to warm their soul.

She had just walked towards the window, finally ready to flip the sign, officially ending her workday, when the door breezed open, the tiny bell overhead chiming.

"I'm sorry, we're closed," she said, looking to her left, in the direction of the door.

"What? No. You can't be, not yet." The stranger lifted his arm, revealing a watch. "It's still five to nine."

She heaved a sigh. "Maybe your watch is slow?"

He laughed. "It's not. And I swear I wouldn't be in here unless it was an emergency."

"An emergency?" Walking towards the stranger, she marveled at how tall he was. Even with her heels, he had at least three inches on her. He wore black dress pants, a blue shirt, and a black coat over top.

"Yes, you see, I just have to have a latte. My life depends on it."

This caused her to laugh. "That might be true, but I've already closed up the till."

Taking a step forward, he came more into the light, a frown playing on his lips. "You would seriously do that? Deny a dying man his last wish?" Then he said, "What's your name?"

There was a nametag, pinned to her shirt, resting over her heart, and yet, he hadn't seemed to notice it. He was looking at her. Really looking at her, and not the parts of her body she would cover up if she could.

Ethan hesitated. What was her name? He typed a few out, but then deleted them promptly, none of them sounding quite right, or fitting the character he imagined, not suiting her. Then, he heard another whisper. So close, breath touching his ear, that he turned to look behind him, sure there must have been someone standing over his shoulder. It felt that real. And then he knew.

"Lilah. My name's Lilah."

He held out his hand. "My name's Chris."

When his hand touched her, she felt a tingle shoot up her arm but was unable to tear her eyes away from him, captured by his gaze. Eyes the color of the autumn leaves outside. Yellow and brown tinged, with hints of green clinging to them. She was enticed by the shape of his mouth, and lips; a slight grin playing on them. His hair was cut short, and Lilah wondered if it was as soft to the touch as it looked, resisting the urge to reach out and feel him.

"Well, Lilah, what if I offer to buy you a latte, too? Would that get me one?"

How could she say no? There was something that wedged itself into Lilah's heart, and she knew, if she turned him away, she might always regret it. Things happened for a reason, Lilah believed, and she had to go with her gut and take a chance. Risking the unknown.

Satisfaction curled a smile on his face. This was what Lilah wanted. His character, she wanted a love story. More than a love story. And he continued to write, the next hours passing without thought as he found he was just as enthralled with the romance that had begun to form, eager to see what would happen next. She needed not only a handsome man, but someone that would sweep her off her feet. Taking the time to worship her. Ethan had been that kind of guy once, but he lost himself along the way. He didn't think he could ever be the kind of man Lilah needed and it killed him a little, even if she wasn't real.

Three dates with Chris had passed by in a blur, and he had yet to lean in for a single chaste kiss. He held her hand, tightly like he'd been worried that if he didn't, he would lose her. She needed to know what it would be like. He'd taken things slowly, expressing his need to make sure she was comfortable, willing, and ready. She was. She knew it. She could no longer wait to have that first kiss, to know if it would be everything she wanted. Perfection. Firsts always were. They were the basis that everything was built on. They had already developed a strong connection, but that wasn't enough for Lilah. She needed Chris to give himself over completely.

When it finally came, Chris cradled her face in his hands. He leaned in, just enough to brush his lips against hers. Lilah shivered at the feather-light touch, yet the anticipation igniting the blood in her veins. She gripped him tightly, palming his shirt in her hands, pulling him closer. He deepened the kiss, at first gently, but then, sweeping his soft tongue against hers, pressing with eagerness, as if to ask for permission. She sighed. Her own lips parting, allowing her to taste him.

Ethan knew he had done her proud, because even he felt the effects within him, sadly pining for that kind of moment of his own. And he made sure that although the kiss was flawless, that each one after was given to Lilah with the same amount of ardor and passion as the first. In fact, it was the same devotion that he felt for her, that pushed him to the next level. He hadn't meant ever, for a story to take on a direction, other than a simplistic and pure romance, but he couldn't contain himself. He was unable to quell the voice inside him. It begged for his fingers to type faster, to progress the story, push Chris and Lilah over the brink. Hell-bent on filling them with even more passion than before. But she had to wait. There was more to be told.

The day had turned into night, and Ethan ignored the strain in his fingers. He had taken minimal breaks, avoiding anything that might break the concentration of the story and the spirit it invoked in him. But he knew things were drawing to a close. There was only one more thing this epic love needed. He had been putting it off, a little, throwing a few curve balls that he felt she hadn't liked. The urge to delete some of the words on the page became all consuming. But he hadn't given in. Not all romance was perfect. There were up's and down's and Chris and Lilah needed a few roadblocks to overcome. He also wasn't sure if he could close the deal. He knew how the novella would end, but the nerves had begun to get the best of him. Having stepped way out of his comfort zone in the first place was a change he had been willing to accept, but pushing the boundaries just that bit more had him squirming. She was ready, he knew it, she'd been murmuring in his ear, her voice growing louder, insistent. But could he give her the night that she deserved? Could he write Chris in the manner that would have readers swooning, toes curling? Would he be able to create that moment of pure ecstasy? He would try, at the very least...

It had been a perfect evening. And Lilah wanted nothing more than to be completely consumed by Chris. They were able to take what they had learned about each other, and come out stronger on the other side. Things were going to be tough, Lilah was sure of that. But she was also confident that, even now, she had found him. Her connection. Her forever.

Chris slid is fingers over the delicate waves of Lilah's hair. His hands traveled down her neck, over her shoulders, sliding the straps of her dress free. She gasped as the silky fabric glided to the floor. Swallowing, she refused to feel self-conscious. The longing look in Chris' eyes told her all she needed. She felt safe and secure. And he had always been that. He knew how to put her at ease with a smile or a look, or a caress of his fingers. A hug, when she most needed it. He had seen her both at her worst over the past weeks, and at her best. They had been able to confide their deepest darkest secrets. Lilah had shared with him her worries, her fears, but also about the future she saw for herself, and that she wanted him to be a part of it.

"You're so beautiful," he said, his voice sounding hoarse, as his eyes found hers.

She wasn't sure, but wondered if the raging beats of her heart could be heard by him as he lowered his lips to hers, seizing them. Standing on her tip-toes, she leaned up, pressing the length of her body against his, drawing her arms around his neck. It allowed the kiss to es-

calate, intensifying with each passing second. And when she broke free, reaching for the buttons of his shirt, she missed the affection he had poured into it.

Lilah tugged at the fabric, releasing it from his pants. He reached up, pulling it off and dropping it to the floor of her bedroom. Her hands instantly went to his bare chest, fingers skimming over every inch of his exposed skin, until he captured her hands, taking them into his, pulling her towards the bed.

He sat down at her side, kissing the top of her shoulder, as he tugged at the straps of her bra, bringing it down, revealing the top of one breast, and then the other. Eagerly, she reached back and undid the clasp, releasing the constraint, sending it to the floor. His mouth found her skin again, kissing, a moment later, switching to dragging his tongue over her. Slowly inching closer, lower, until he pulled one of her pert nipples into his mouth, sucking it.

Lilah all but came undone at the feel of his warm mouth teasing the tender skin, and the only thought that crossed her mind was of wanting more, wanting him to overwhelm her with even more sensual touches. Her insides burning, tingling, awoke with the need to be pleasured until she could no longer stand another second. Needing to know what it felt like to have him inside her...

Ethan cleared his throat, having been pulled out of the scene before him as his own arousal became evident, straining against his pants. That had to be a good thing, and so he continued on. He gave Lilah and Chris everything he could. He'd made himself blush, but knew if that were the case, he'd done his job well. Lilah had needed someone to cherish her. That was what she wanted most out of the story that she had told him.

As Ethan wrote the final sentences of the story, he was gripped with a sense of gratitude. Like someone had reached out, touched his shoulders and poured it into him. He typed "The End," saved the file and shut the computer down, feeling accomplished.

When he turned around and got up from the chair, he blinked. Unfocused, maybe, or he had made it up, but at first it was just a glimmer. Then it began to take shape. Ethan pressed his palms into his eyes, rubbing the image away. Only when he reopened them, she was there, he was sure of it, standing right in front of him.

Lilah.

"Thank you," she said, and it was the voice he heard all along. He was certain. He'd have recognized it anywhere. The one telling him the story that had to be written. But just as he opened his mouth to speak, to say something, though he wasn't sure what he might have said, she wiggled her fingers in a wave.

A smile plastered on her face, she dissolved into the air around him.

He stared at the space for a long while until he realized what she was, having been lost without it for so long. But he had found her and had taken her into his soul. She had given back to him the will to write.

She was his muse.

Bookstores and Dreams

HENLEY FLIPPED through the worn and dog-eared pages of "The Write Way" her eyes searching for a line highlighted in yellow. Who was she kidding? The entire book, one of her most prized possessions, was almost entirely highlighted in various fluorescent colors.

Though she had read the book front to back, dozens of times over the years, she often turned to it when sitting at her computer. There was a quote or tip that suited almost every situation, and it always helped her find that voice of inspiration when she needed it.

It had been the last gift her father had given her before he died. She'd toted the book around with her everywhere; stained with coffee, binding torn and barely holding together, and, of course, marked-up and dog-eared. Henley couldn't let the book out of her sight. Not just because it often seemed to give her the courage to write, but what it had stood for; her father's belief in her. That he understood her need to be creative, and that he'd always be there to help.

* * *

Henley could close her eyes, remembering the day so clearly. The book wrapped in glossy paper and given to her just because. A few days before that, she'd declared to her parents that she was going to be a writer. And she'd do whatever it took to achieve that. Her father had seen the sparkle in her eye, as she waved the paper, graded with an A, and he'd told her, "If you want to be a writer, be a writer. And never give up." Henley would also never forget the discouraging look her mother had given the two; trying to ruin the moment by claiming Henley's dream was most likely something unattainable, that Henley would be better suited to a "real" career, like becoming a doctor or a lawyer.

A rift between Henley and her mother had quickly formed, as the bond between her and her father had grown even stronger. The two would stay up late plotting out possible novel ideas, creating characters and magical fantasy realms. Back then, they were mostly short stories. Her father spent countless hours reading every one. At the time, Henley sincerely believed she'd be a writer and that her first novel would be dedicated to her father, and that he'd be around to see it happen. He'd be the first in line to buy a copy, have it signed and display it proudly. However, The Write Way had been the last thing her father ever gave her.

A few months after his gift, he died suddenly of a heart attack, taking Henley's dream of being a writer with him. She'd felt lost without her critique partner, the sadness overwhelming to the point that Henley couldn't even think of writing a single word without breaking down in tears. To Henley, her heart and her mind were blocked, and she'd never succeed without her father at her side cheering her on.

Years later she remembered the book. It had begun to collect dust on the shelf, and one day Henley plucked it from its spot, sat down on her bed, and started to read it. After just a few pages, she'd felt that itch to write. The inspiring how-to guide re-lit the fire Henley had allowed to burn out. Not only did she realize that she still wanted to be a writer, but perhaps part of her knew it was what her father still wanted for her. After all, the inscription on the cover page was in her father's messy scrawl, a mantra she had forgotten. She had given up. As she read through the book, she realized that her father very well might have been looking down on her from heaven—if there was such a place—with disappointment in his eyes. Henley couldn't bear that thought. Once she'd inhaled all the book had to offer, she found herself sitting at her computer typing out the words to her first novel. Even if her father wasn't there to see it, she had to show herself that she still had what it would take. She could be whatever she wanted, and deep down, she still desperately wanted to be a novelist.

Between her college classes, her part-time job, and life, Henley wrote. It took her more than a year, and a lot of hard work, but soon she'd typed "The End" on her first novel. She'd felt satisfied and genuinely proud of herself. The words of her father and the words of the book were the muse that kept her going. The whisper in her ear that told her never to give up. And Henley felt that as long as she had the book, the whisper would never fade. Over the next year it had motivated her to write two more novels. She'd even begun to think that what she had could be something publishable and begun to pursue just that.

While she learned everything she'd needed to know about the literary industry, editing and re-editing those first few novels, Henley continued to write. The voices— the muse—inside her, overflowed her with ideas that were desperate to end up on the pages of upcoming novels. She had more ideas than she knew what to do with and worried about how she'd possibly ever find the time to write them all down. Along with the inspiring how-to book Henley constantly carried with her, she also brought along a notepad and pen. No matter where she was or what she was doing, she was able to write down the whims of the muse. Filling notebook after notebook with novel ideas, characters, and continuing to create worlds outside of her own. She hadn't settled on a genre, an age group, anything. She just wrote what seemed to be the loudest idea coming from her brain, whether it was an adventurous tale of knights and dragons, bloodthirsty vampires or romance hungry vixens. Nothing was off limits.

To Henley's dismay, her mother had moved on, perhaps a little too quickly. Or at least, it felt that way. Soon, her mother had gotten remarried and started a new family. The rift that began that day in the kitchen, when she'd looked down at Henley and her dream, had since become a gorge. The Grand Canyon. When Henley declared her choice of college, and her major would be literature, it had become apparent that some damages could never be repaired.

Though they say time may heal all wounds, for Henley, the loss of her father still weighed heavy on her heart. A cut just as fresh as the day she'd been told he'd never give her another hug. Read another one of her stories. Or be there when she needed him most.

After a few years of only seeing her mother on holidays, when she couldn't come up with an excuse that would get her out of attending, her mother called out of the blue. She had been desperate to see her first daughter, and had insisted she'd come to terms with Henley's choices. Henley reluctantly agreed to see her, willing to make an effort to patch up the gaping holes in their fragile relationship.

* * *

Henley waited at the café, searching her book for a particular passage, scanning the words, thumbing through the pages. She'd been making notes when she hit a wall on her latest project. Whenever Henley struggled, she pulled out her literary Bible, often instantly spurring her with a renewed sense of eagerness and inspiration to push through. Her heel tapped against the floor, knee bouncing as she grew impatient with herself, and her mother, who was already more than fifteen minutes late.

Just when she'd begun to give up hope, Henley found what she was looking for: a quote by a renowned author about character building. She read it, letting the words wrap around her like a security blanket. Letting the voice whisper in her ear, creating that moment of awe where the pieces she'd been missing began to weave together in her mind.

"Seriously, Henley? Couldn't you have left that damn book at home? You know how I—"

Henley peered over the pages of the book with a scowl. Her mother, Abigail, was standing just to her left, having appeared almost out of nowhere.

"If it bothers you, Abigail, you know where the door is," Henley replied with a huff of annoyance, using the book to gesture the door at the far end of the café. "Perhaps if you weren't late," she glanced at her watch, "I wouldn't have had to pull it out of my bag in the first place."

Still standing, Abigail was the picture of poise and elegance. She wore a well-tailored gray pantsuit and blazer. Her brown hair was pulled up into a chignon that hid the silvery strands that had begun to take over. Even her makeup was flawless. But heavier than Henley had remembered her ever wearing. She took her new role as a wealthy wife to rich-ass business man a little too seriously. There was a time when people said the two looked alike, but Henley could hardly recognize the woman standing before her.

"Please, Henley, enough with the dramatics. I'm a few minutes late, the driver couldn't find a parking spot and had to circle around."

"Fine. See. I'm putting the book away." Henley gathered up her notepad, pen, and her prized book, and shoved them into the bag that hung on the back of the chair. "Now please, Mother, I'm dying to hear why you so urgently needed to see me." She motioned carelessly to the chair opposite her, permitting her mother to take a seat, though Henley knew she needn't bother. Her mother was going to take a seat, regardless of how much Henley was already regretting the impromptu mother-daughter bonding session.

With her nose clearing tipped to the sky, Abigail delicately sat down, perfect posture and smug expression. She was quiet, eerily so, for what felt like an eternity. Henley saw a few different emotions flash through her eyes and over her face. Then, though she wouldn't have believed it were possible, Abigail sniffled. She took a napkin from the dispenser on the table and dabbed at the corner of her eyes.

"This is hard for me, to come here, like this, but—"

"Please, God, just spit it out," Henley said, sitting now at the edge of her seat. No matter how much she disliked her mother, the pang of guilt in her stomach was loud and clear at the sight of Abigail suddenly so distressed. She cared. Even if she hadn't wanted to; wished she could look at the person sitting across from her and see a stranger, and not the mother who'd raised her.

"It's Hailey, honey. She's sick."

It felt like someone punched Henley in the stomach. "What-what do you mean, sick?" Obviously, her mother's urgent need to see Henley meant that it wasn't a cold, a flu bug, but rather, something more.

Using the napkin to draw away more tears, Abigail replied, "Cancer, honey. My baby has cancer." She burst into a fit of hysterics.

"Oh, God, Mom. I'm so sorry," Henley replied, feeling terrible. More than terrible. She hadn't exactly been the older sister Hailey probably deserved, and was overly callous when it came to matters that involved her mother. Now, that pang of guilt morphed into gut-wrenching turmoil. "What... what can I do?" Henley added, knowing there probably wasn't anything. It wasn't as though she secretly held the cure to cancer in her pocket. Though she wished she had. Her sister, Hailey, was barely five years old. She had her whole life ahead of her. Too young to be taken away. Not to mention, Henley wasn't sure she could fathom the loss of another person dear to her.

Pulling herself together, Abigail responded, her tone a little hopeful, "Well, there is something..." her voice trailed off. Turning her attention to the expensive purse she held in her lap, Abigail loosened the clasp and pulled free some papers, sliding them across the table.

Henley read, her eyebrows dipping in question. "Permission forms?"

"Yes. To be tested. Hailey needs a bone marrow transplant. Her father and I aren't a match, but-but they said you might be."

"Aren't there people who donate that sort of thing? I mean, just like donating blood..."

"Yes, of course. And Hailey is on the waiting list. But the transplant has a better success rate if... Well if... It comes from a matched family member."

Inhaling a deep breath, Henley looked down at the papers. The foreign medical jargon began to blur her vision. "When?"

"If you sign the papers, we can go to the hospital now."

Henley looked away from her mother's optimistic expression, zeroing her attention on an abstract painting on the far wall. She tried to filter the millions of questions and concerns that invaded her thoughts. But then she remembered something important. Hailey. This was about her, and not Abigail. If Henley did this, she'd be potentially saving a life. Her sister's. How could she not entertain the idea? How could she say no? How could she not do whatever she could to help?

In an instant, Henley realized how hard it must have been for Abigail to come to her. Desperate. Worried. She'd lost someone already, as had Henley. She suddenly felt sympathetic as she grabbed the bag from the back of the chair.

"Wait. Before you leave. Just—think about it. Please. I know it's a lot to ask. But—"

Henley raised her hand, silencing her mother.

"I'm just getting a pen."

Abigail put her hand over her heart, eyes welling with fresh tears. "Oh, thank God."

"She's my sister. I'll do whatever I can to help." Henley signed on the line, giving permission to have her bone marrow tested to see if it would be a match to Hailey's. She had watched enough medical dramas on TV to know a little bit about the procedure and how painful it would be. That pain wouldn't compare to the loss that would consume her if she sat back and did nothing, letting her sister die.

"My driver's outside waiting. We can go to the hospital now and the doctors can explain everything to you. Can you do that?"

"Yeah, Mom, I can do that."

Abigail stood, just as Henley did. She reached forward and pulled her daughter into a hug. Henley was reluctant to return the sentiment, but found herself wrapping her arms around her mother. Abigail slumped with relief as if clinging on to the hope that this would be what Hailey needed to get better.

Henley had driven to the café. She fed the meter with all her change, before walking over to the sleek black sedan that idled at the curb just a few spots away. The image fit with her mother, impeccably dressed with an air of elegance, but Henley felt awkward as she climbed into the back. She wasn't used to such a luxury. She'd rarely taken cabs, preferring to save money by walking. Even her own car often sat untouched in the parking lot.

Her mother talked endlessly about Hailey's condition; how it had been detected almost a year before, but had progressively gotten worse. Henley only half-listened, clutching her bag, allowing her book to give her the comfort and strength she needed. She even felt a few ideas prickling the back of her neck, the book and her father working their magic. Though she resisted the urge to pull out her notepad in front of Abigail and make a few notes. Instead, Henley concentrated on the view from the window.

What Henley heard first was the driver yelling, "Hang on!" and then the screeching tires. Henley drew her attention forward, leaning in her seat for a better view just as a Semi-truck jackknifed in the middle of the freeway. By the time Henley realized what was coming, it was too late. The sound of crunching metal, the impact, her bag no longer in her hands, but seized by imaginary fingers, came an instant later. Henley tried to brace herself. But then she was falling, consumed by blackness as an excruciating amount of pain spiraled from her head, down her back, to the tips of her toes. The wind knocked from her lungs.

* * *

Henley woke with a splitting headache, throbbing behind blurred eyes. Her throat was sore, dry and parched. She coughed as she'd begun to adjust to her surroundings.

"Easy. The doctors had to give you some strong sedatives."

Lazily, Henley turned her head to the side.

"I'm so glad you're awake," Abigail said, perched on the edge of a chair, hand firmly grasped to Henley's. She wore different clothes than last Henley had seen her. She looked more like the woman who had raised her, wearing simple jeans and fitted t-shirt. But it was the sling holding her arm in place that grabbed Henley's attention, as she thought back to the last thing she remembered. They had been on their way to the hospital when they were... In a car accident.

"What-what happened?"

"Oh, honey, a truck driver fell asleep at the wheel and hit us. We're lucky to be alive."

Instinctively, Henley began to flex her muscles, assessing the damage as she lifted her hands to her head. A bandage covered her forehead and shooting pain raced up her leg when she tried to wiggle the toes on her right foot.

"You had a nasty bump on the head. Some swelling in the brain. It was touch and go for a bit, honey, but you'll be fine. The doctors have assured me."

Henley tried to sit up as she said, "My-my leg hurts."

"It's not too bad. Could be worse, really. Just a small fracture. You'll have the cast on for a few weeks."

That didn't seem too serious, in retrospect. She was alive. Though, had she been wearing her seatbelt, Henley might have been better off. It was then Henley remembered the point of the car ride in the first place.

"Hailey."

Abigail waved her hand in the air. "She's fine, honey. Great, actually. They were able to do the transplant last week, thanks to you being a near-perfect match."

"Last week?" Panic began to eclipse the throb in her head and the ache in her leg. She hadn't remembered any procedures. Hell, she hadn't remembered getting to the hospital after the accident. Those events were veiled with a thick fog Henley couldn't see through.

"Don't panic-" her mother began. Henley snorted. She was already doing just that. "But you've been in here three weeks. We pulled some strings, and, well, we figured it'd be better just to go ahead with the procedures, honey, since you'd already signed the permission forms."

That made sense. Probably better not having to remember that. But three weeks!

"School." Henley swallowed. "My job..."

Again, Abigail waved her hand in the air as if those things didn't matter. "I took care of those. You're going to be out of commission for a little bit. I've got your professors sending over your work, and with the semester almost over, and summer just around the corner... Well, I thought, maybe you'd want to come home—come home with me so I can take care of you..."

Henley could hear the sincerity in her mother's tone, not to mention, as they had in the café, her blue eyes began to well with tears.

"Please. Let me do this for you." At Henley's apparent hesitation, she quickly added, "How about you think about it? You don't have to make up your mind right now. I-I'll go get the doctor."

Abigail sashayed across the small hospital room and out the door. The click the door made when it closed behind Abigail was loud. Foreboding. Henley turned on her side, pressing her cheek against the hard hospital pillow. Tears pooled in her eyes and slipped down her cheeks. She hated the position she was in. There was no clear option, not one that would make things easier, on either of them. Abigail may have wanted to step up, now, after all this time, and be a mother to her again, but Henley was reluctant. However, with a broken leg, a bump on her head, and no work to pay her bills, she didn't have much of a choice.

A few days later, Henley was released from the hospital and into the care of her mother. It had become clear she needed help. Simple things like getting from the hospital bed to the washroom were a chore, not to mention, the doctor wouldn't let her leave alone. She had to rely on someone. Her options were severely limited. Abigail, however, was taking on her new role with more enthusiasm than Henley was comfortable with.

"Here, I brought you this," Abigail said, passing over a simple sundress. "I hope it fits." She bit her bottom lip, as she turned around and waited for Henley to slip out of the backless hospital gown and into the dress. Henley was thankful it was summer. Dresses and shorts would be so much easier with a cast.

"You can turn around," Henley said, sliding from the bed, resting her weight on the crutches she'd begun to get very familiar with.

Abigail smiled with delight. "It's perfect."

"Are you sure this is what you want? I mean, you have Hailey to take care of..."

"Hailey won't be released from the hospital for another week or two. They want to keep a close eye on her, make sure there are no infections or... Her immune system is just so delicate, right now."

Inhaling a deep breath, Henley said, "Okay. Let's do this." Then she looked around. "Where's my bag?" She hadn't thought about it at all, but suddenly it hit her, she hadn't seen it. Not since the day of the accident, having it held tightly in her lap.

"Um, well... It didn't make it, honey. They'd just barely gotten us out of the car when..."

Henley shook her head in dismay. "What do you mean it didn't make it?"

"The car went up in flames, Henley. There's nothing left."

The air was knocked from Henley's lungs as she fought for a breath, slumping against the bed. *No!* she screamed in her head. "Are you sure? I mean... It can't be gone!"

"Henley, it's just a book. It's not the end of the—"

"Dammit! It's not just a book." She gulped in breaths of air, feeling woozy. Her hands slipped from the crutches. They fell to the floor as Henley wrapped her arms around her stomach. She felt as though she was going to be sick. "That-that's all I have left of him!"

"That's not true. At all. You have what's in your heart. You don't need a book—"

Going from feeling sick to angry, Henley said, "It was more than a book, *Mother*," she spat the word. "It was... everything!" Henley closed her eyes, concentrating as hard as she could, eager to hear the whisper, the muse, inside her soul. It wasn't there. Only silence met her. Come to think of it, Henley thought, she hadn't had any new ideas since she'd come to. No itch to write. No... It couldn't be gone, could it?

"No, honey, it wasn't. And we'll get you a new one. If it means that much to you, we'll find another copy. It's not a big deal."

But it was. It was a huge deal. Henley believed that the book—the last connection she felt she had with her father—was the reason for the constant fill of endless concepts just waiting to be written. Ever since she'd sat down to read the book, all those years ago, and carrying it around with her since, she never, never struggled with ideas, or something to write about. They were always just there. Loud and clear, and infinite.

Of course, Abigail didn't see that. Couldn't under-stand. At that moment, it felt as though a piece of Henley was missing. It wasn't just the book, but rather, a void in her heart, a flaw in her soul, the loss of some-thing that had become what Henley thought was a permanent fixture in her life. Writing, those ideas, and her father were what made Henley who she was, and who she aspired to become. And without those things, she felt, again, as though she'd begun to let down the dream they had shared together. It was the one thing she knew, if she tried hard enough and didn't give up, was attainable. The only hope she had was that it wasn't going to be a lasting mark on herself. That perhaps, given some time, the desire and passion for writing would come back, full force.

Henley calmed herself down. "Sure. Okay. We'll find another copy."

* * *

The weeks passed by in a blur, between physiotherapy once she got her cast off, and the incessant babying from her mother and the complete and utter lack of voice in her head . . . Henley was ready to get back to her life. To begin to decide how she was going to get through the rest of it, if her one and only dream had now become unattainable. Henley had spent her time on her mother's expensive couch, leg in the air, sifting through the files on her computer. She flipped through the pages of the notebooks she retrieved from her apartment, praying she'd be able to find the will to write. She read and re-read everything she had ever laid down on paper—tidbits of plots, character demographics, random lines of dialog—and yet, nothing came to her. Not a whisper, not an inkling, not that familiar tingle in her stomach when she got excited and couldn't wait to get to work.

She started to believe her muse was trapped in the disintegrated book. And now that she didn't have it, she'd never be able to pick up those pieces and work on another novel. She couldn't bear the thought of disappointing her father, from beyond the grave, yet Henley couldn't figure out how to get it back.

Abigail had painstakingly done what she could to track down another copy of the book. Though Henley knew it wouldn't quite be the same. It would be missing that familiar scrawl of her father's writing on the page; where she'd brushed her fingers over the indentations; could close her eyes and remember each curve of his letters, how he'd pressed down harder, deepening the blue ink and the impression it made, when he'd written the words "Don't give up."

The new book would lack the adventures she'd taken it on, carrying it with her through the final years of high school. And on a road trip she'd taken with some girlfriends where they turned around and drove two hours back to a small diner where she'd left her purse. She remembered what it had felt like—not knowing if the book would be inside. To her relief, it was still there. Henley had also carried the book with her to the hospital after her half-sister, Hailey, was born, and how reading it in the waiting room sparked a few ideas. A new book wouldn't hold those same memories, or that mumble of constant encouragement, which came from her father. He'd been the one to believe in her right from the start. But Henley wasn't willing to give up hope entirely.

Although, as it would turn out, the book—long since out of print—was written by an author who produced that one and only piece. It was impossible to come by. Searches of the internet came up empty. A rather nasty phone call to the publisher ended with Abigail finally giving up as they no longer held the rights to the work and weren't interested in helping her find a copy. Henley did what she could, but she supposed when you only wrote one book, selling a less than spectacular amount, it would be easy to drop off the face of the earth and become a recluse. Her only hope was finding it wedged on a shelf of a used bookstore. But that was like searching for a needle in a haystack. Henley called dozens of them and most hadn't even heard of the book or the author, and were unable to help her.

As time wore on, Henley accepted she'd never be the same without finding the book that had inspired her. Would never be taught another lesson she needed to know in order to craft, what she thought, were brilliant works of fiction. It was just another thing that had her life spiraling slowly out of control, quickly losing sight of who she was.

Yet, every time Henley walked past a bookstore, she had to go in. It was like they were a beacon, calling to her, and she couldn't move on without at least knowing. Without looking. It became like a nervous habit. Just the possibility of finding the book gave her the shakes, tingling her body, speeding up her heart rate. The anxiety was overwhelming. Something she assumed was similar to a drug addict searching for their next fix; an unfortunate comparison, maybe, but the truth. She'd stop whatever she was doing just to go inside.

On a particularly hard day, Henley found herself driving several hours in one direction, just to get away. She had discovered Abigail's way of "taking care of her" was putting in her resignation at the café where she waited tables. It also meant giving up the lease on the apartment she'd secured for herself, a few short blocks away from her school. And even though she had gotten the missing assignments from Henley's professors, Abigail had begun to nudge and nag her into accepting a different direction in life. Abigail suddenly wanted full control over her affairs. She'd offered to pay the tuition for her college courses if she chose a different major. Was willing to help her find another apartment, closer to where Abigail lived, and would pay for that, too. She said it was so Henley could concentrate on her education. Naturally, so she could secure a new, more realistic, career option. Or better yet, she'd allow Henley to live, for free, in the tiny guest house on the property her mother owned.

Henley was suffocating. The deceit and the lies she had been told built up to the point that Henley couldn't take it. She couldn't look her mother in the eyes without seeing hatred. She knew her mom was a force, and almost always got what she wanted, but to manipulate her daughter... Henley was disgusted. And she hated the day she had ever gotten into a car with her mother, that moment having been the catalyst that began to unravel her entire life.

As the sky overhead began to darken, and Henley still feeling no better over the outburst she and her mother had hours before, she took the next exit, which made way to a small town. Part of her knew she should probably find a gas station, fuel up, grab some snacks and make the long journey back home, but she couldn't do it; couldn't bring herself to pull into the gas station, and passed by it without much thought. Her mother would still be furious. Hell, Henley was crazed with anger over her mother believing she could tempt her into making drastic changes, and throw money at any problem, just to make it better.

Instead, Henley found Main Street, the tiny shops, cafés and restaurants still aglow with tourists enjoying the summer holidays. She pulled into an angled spot and cut the engine, only to rest her head against the steering wheel, breathing deeply. A few minutes later, she shoved open the door, the humid air of the hot summer night surrounding her instantly. It felt good. Being someplace else. Far, far away from her controlling mother and her broken dreams.

Though she'd graduated from having to use crutches, Henley still walked with a less-than-graceful gait; the pain in her leg a dull pestering ache that might never go away. Another perpetual reminder of how wrong she'd been about seeing her mother. She'd helped Hailey, but it was the only small glimmer of light that made it okay. It was also why Abigail was so sure that Henley would bend to her will. She couldn't walk or stand for extended periods of time; still many hours of therapy ahead of her, and medical bills left unpaid, making her employment options limited.

Henley ambled up the street, stopping abruptly at the corner. On the other side was a used bookstore. She scrutinized the list in her mind of all the stores in the area that she called in search of her elusive muse. The name, Re: Read Books, came to mind, and Henley hesitated for only a moment before crossing the street, making a beeline for the store. There was that slight chance, no matter how small, and Henley couldn't pass it up. She'd pulled into the town, parked and got out to stretch her legs, but also to get her mind to focus on something else. The hope that propelled her forward was enough of a reason to open the door and go inside.

Henley inhaled deeply. The dimly lit store cased shelves and shelves of books. They were stacked on the tops, lining the floor in teetering piles, resting on tables, and underneath them. The smell, that musk of old leather bindings, dust and something else, was calming.

"Can I help you find something?"

A man popped out from behind a stack of books, clutching a few titles in his hand as he looked warmly towards her with a friendly smile. It caught her attention immediately. It was an honest smile, and as he set the books down and came towards her, Henley couldn't help but be drawn by the way he carried himself. He was full of masculine features. A toned body underneath a snug t-shirt and jeans slung low on his hips. Tattoos covered his arms. Henley could make out the etchings of books with wings, which disappeared beneath the

128

fabric. His hair was cut short, a bronzy brown, held in place by gel. Severe features of an angular jaw were clean shaven. But his eyes, the closer he came to her, drew her attention further. A soft blue you could get lost in, that held all kinds of emotion and secrets, even a hint of sadness.

Her heart picked up pace, rumbling inside her chest. Henley wasn't sure if it was because of the man or the buildup of anticipation of finally finding the book. It would seem almost fitting, Henley thought, that it could potentially find its way back to her when she needed it most. Having that book might easily be the thing that helped her decide the rest of her future.

Then, ignoring the slim chances, Henley pushed that aside, suddenly so sure that the store owner would have it. She'd have bet her life on it. She needed the book so badly, she wasn't willing to believe that it might not be among the hundreds of others.

"Um, yeah. Maybe. I'm wondering if you have a copy of a book called, "The Write Way." It's sort of a how-to guide. By an author named Trent Holbrook."

Henley could have sworn there was a flicker of recognition in his alluring eyes, and yet after an excruciating amount time, he replied, "No. I don't think I do."

Nodding, while holding her disappointment at bay, Henley responded with a quick, "Alright. Thanks," and turned to leave. She'd made it a few steps when a splinter of pain shot up her leg, causing her to stumble, just as what felt like the weight of the world came crashing down on her. She'd been so sure. Positive. And yet, she couldn't think past the moment, and how much hurt suddenly wrenched at her heart, mirroring what she felt from her no longer broken leg.

"Hey, easy there," she heard the man say.

But all Henley couldn't think about was getting away from the books, the man, and her life before the dam she'd built up broke. She wanted to have a choice when she released the flood of emotions that were building so forcefully inside her, and it certainly wasn't going to be in the company of a stranger. It all wasn't just about the book, or her father, even Abigail; it was about how lost she suddenly felt. Alone.

Henley took a few calculated steps towards the door; her leg hell-bent on giving out on her, as tears began to burn her eyes, blurring her vision. She hated how weak it made her feel. And she'd almost made it to the door when a sob involuntary pierced through the air.

A second later, a strong hand slipped into hers, pulling her back. "Wait. Please. Is everything okay?" He turned her around, just as the first few tears managed to slip free and roll down Henley's cheeks.

She couldn't find the words, her lips pressed in a tight line, chin quivering as a few more tears spilled free. Instead, she shook her head. No. She wasn't okay. If that hadn't already been abundantly clear.

"Here, why don't you... Sit down for a moment, okay." He tugged lightly on her hand and began walking just a few steps from the door where a chair rested, covered in books. Without a thought, the man swept them to the floor with a thud.

Slumping into the chair, Henley put her head in her hands, hiding herself. She had hoped he would just leave her be, alone, crying in a chair, surrounded by books, hours away from home but that wasn't the case.

"Here, take this," he said. When Henley looked up, he was kneeling on the ground in front of her. He pulled a square handkerchief from his pocket. "It's clean, I swear." It was an odd sight, and something that didn't seem to suit the tough guy persona that encompassed him. Had she saw him on the street, she wouldn't have thought he'd be the curator of bookstore either.

Henley took the hanky and forced a smile. She dabbed at her eyes and inhaled a shaky breath.

"Do you want to tell me what's wrong?" He looked up at her through long lashes.

A flush of embarrassment heated her cheeks further. "Not really."

He lifted his chin slowly. "Sure. Okay. Well, I was just about to close. If you give me a minute, I can help you home."

At the mention of home, Henley shed a few more tears of frustration. The absolute last place she wanted to go was back to Abigail's. She'd rather sleep in her car if she had to. "I-I'm not from around here."

"Oh. Well, where you from?" Then he said, "My name's Garret, by the way." He held out his hand, and Henley took it. He grasped firmly, touch lingering, sending another blush to work over her face and neck.

"I'm Henley," she responded, his hand still laced with hers. "I sort of just drove here. Needed to get away. I live in Castlegar."

Garret whistled. "And you came all the way here?"

She shrugged. "I just drove. Trying to clear my head, I guess."

"Alright." He stood up. "How about I make you a cup of coffee? Might perk you up before you have to drive all the way back."

It was a nice gesture. Thoughtful. But Henley looked between Garret and the door, apprehensively.

"I promise. I'm a good guy. Not that my word means much. But I'll be a complete gentleman. I swear," he said.

It was more than two hours home, in the dark, on a two lane highway. Though she'd been able to get back into a car after her accident, she still felt uneasy about being behind the wheel. That, she'd been told, would just take time. But it also meant that the idea of driving back wasn't an appealing thought.

"Okay. That sounds nice."

"Great. Follow me," he said over his shoulder as he began to walk away. Henley stood on shaky legs and pushed herself to keep up as he disappeared into the towering stacks of books. He weaved through them effortlessly, occasionally flipping his gaze over his shoulder, just to make sure she was still keeping up, until they were at the far end of the store, staring down a door.

He pushed it open to reveal a stock room and a rickety old staircase. "My apartment is just up here," he motioned to the area above them.

Clutching the handkerchief tightly in her hand, Henley climbed the stairs, which led to another door at the top. Once inside, Henley marveled at the amount of books kept hidden up there. The store could have had an entire second floor of merchandise. They were crammed into every nook, covering every surface, save for a small ledge of counter in the kitchen area, and a bed at the other end of the space. There was an ornate table and chairs, and Garret was quick to say, "Sit down and I'll put the coffee on. It'll only take a minute."

She did as he'd said, and sat down. He pulled a bag of coffee from the freezer, filled the pot with water, and flicked the switch. He kept a close eye on the coffee that sputtered from the maker as he leaned against the counter. Or perhaps, he was just giving Henley some space. Either way, she was happy to have him not so close in proximity. She didn't deny herself the opportunity to look, letting her eyes sweep over him. He was handsome, without a doubt, and she felt the faintest hint of butterflies in her stomach.

* * *

They stayed silent for a long while, the only sound, Henley's constant heartbeat—loud in her ears—and the coffee machine percolating. When it was done, he grabbed two mugs from a cupboard. "I don't have any cream. Or milk, for that matter. Or sugar. I hope that's okay."

"I take my coffee black, so you're in luck." She smiled and admired how easily the words and emotion came out. She was beginning to feel better.

"Well, if that's the case, we can definitely be friends."

This time, it wasn't just a smile, but laughter too, that came from Henley, catching her a little off guard. But she liked the effortlessness of being with Garret. Bizarrely enough, it didn't feel quite like they were strangers.

He came to her side and set down the coffee before taking a seat across from her. Henley took a tentative sip, testing the flavor and the temperature. It was nearly perfect.

"So, I'm curious, what does one want with a how-to guide that's been out of print for more than a decade?"

Henley's eyes grew wide. "So you've heard of it? Are you a writer?" That was more than she could say about the dozens of bookstore owners she'd talked to. Most didn't recognize the author or the title.

"I dabble, here and there. And yeah, I've heard of it. Grossly under-recognized, if you ask me. What about you?"

With another sip of her coffee, Henley swallowed, taking the time to formulate her reply. "I used to think I was."

His eyebrows pinched together. "That's an odd thing to say. You either are or you're not. I dabble. So yeah,

I'm a writer. Because I write things down. Well, things other than grocery lists."

"I've sort of lost the ability to write things down, other than grocery lists. I used to think I'd never have enough time to work through all the ideas that came to me, and now I can't hear them."

"And you think 'The Write Way' will help you get it back?" At Henley's nod, he added, "Excuse me for saying this, but, that's probably the silliest thing I've ever heard."

Henley frowned.

"No. I don't mean... Well, I kind of do, but hear me out. I think either you're a writer or you're not. And I don't believe it's humanly possible to just wake up one day and not know how to do that. How to push your passion on to the page. I think you can write without the voices. Or rather, you just have to figure out how to get them back."

"Maybe that's true," Henley said solemnly. "Then I just don't know how to get it back." Only to add quickly, "Can we talk about something else?"

She watched Garret take a gulp of his coffee. "Sure."

They fell into conversation about books and Garret. How the bookstore had been his father's and he'd taken it over when he passed away. Henley's heart tugged at the wound still fresh within Garret. That must have been the sadness that she could see in his soft, blue eyes.

He offered her a refill on her coffee, and Henley eagerly accepted. She was enjoying the company of Garret, not wanting the moment to end. From within the pocket of her shorts, though, came a reminder of how she'd ended up at Garret's in the first place. She pulled her ringing phone free and silenced the call from her mother.

"Someone missing you? A boyfriend perhaps?"

It was hard to ignore the suggestive tone in Garret's voice, or the look he gave her as he waited for a response.

"No. No boyfriend." She drained the last of her coffee, only to yawn in the next second. "But I should probably get going. I don't want to overstay."

"I'm not sure I can let you leave, Henley. I may have filled you full of caffeine, but that's not going to be enough of a jolt to get you back to Castlegar. I'd be worried you'd fall asleep at the wheel or something. I can't—I can't have that on my conscience. I can take you to a hotel if you want, or-or you could just stay. Here. With me."

He was probably right. Henley knew that. But she looked at the small double bed, and back towards Garret. She knew she could use one of the credit cards in her purse to pay for a night in a hotel. That wasn't the problem. The issue, the internal struggle Henley was having, was that she wanted to stay with him. She couldn't describe the feeling completely, or why she was so sure that's what she wanted, but she still wasn't ready to let him go.

"I can stay on the floor. If that's what you're wondering about. Seriously. My intentions are nothing but honest."

136

Henley yawned again but tried to cover it up with a cough as she stretched out her arms. "Okay. Sure. That's probably a better idea, anyway. I can't really afford a night in a hotel."

"So it's settled." Garret got up, taking the empty coffee cups back into the kitchen, depositing them in the sink. Next he walked to a closed door Henley hadn't noticed before. A linen closet. He pulled out a few very fluffy and soft-looking blankets and a spare pillow. With a silly grin, he said, "It's been awhile since I had a sleepover. I'm kind of excited. I might even be game for a pillow fight or something. If you want."

Laughing, Henley got up. Her muscles were stiff, and she ambled towards where he'd begun to set up his makeshift bed, just to the left of the real one. He gave her a look, a question playing on his lips, but thankfully, he didn't ask what was wrong with her leg. And he didn't seem to care much about it once she reached for the pillow, taking it from his hands. She hit him lightly with it. "I'm not sure I know you well enough for a pillow fight."

"That's probably true."

She helped Garret get set up. And then stood awkwardly at the foot of the bed, not sure what to do next. He went to a small dresser under one of the windows of the apartment and began pulling a few things free.

"The bathroom is just through there." He lifted his arms up, filled with clothes, in the direction of a door, just off from the kitchen. "I don't know... well... If you want to change into something more comfortable." He held out a pair of sweatpants and a t-shirt.

"I'd like that. Thank you." She took the clothes and disappeared into the bathroom. It was small; a sink, and shower, toilet, and very few personal touches. There was a razor on the ledge, a toothbrush in a small cup. When Henley opened the medicine cabinet, relief washed over her. Nothing out of the ordinary, really. A box of bandages. Some Tylenol. But then, there, suddenly glaring back at her was an unopened box of condoms. It took her a minute to ignore them and tell herself that it wasn't a big deal. It was better to be prepared... Than not. And she'd often kept a few handy, just in case. Though more often than not, they weren't used. She kept to herself mostly, concentrating on school work, knowing there was plenty of time for guys when she'd achieved some of her goals.

Quickly she changed and opened the door. She let out a sharp gasp. Garret was standing by the bed, wearing only a pair of boxers and a t-shirt, which he'd been lifting over his head when he abruptly stopped, his eyes widening at the sight of Henley. "I can... leave this on, if you want." But something told her that wasn't what he'd been thinking. At all. There was definitely an expression that gave her more butterflies.

"It's fine. However you're comfortable."

He pulled the shirt the rest of the way off and tossed it to the floor. He stood for a second, and Henley cursed herself for checking out his toned torso and the dozens of tattoos that covered almost every inch of his skin. She'd noticed the flying books on his arm, but that didn't even cover it. There were what looked like quotes in all different scripts, insignia like Sherlock's trademark pipe and hat. A pair of circular, dark-rimmed spectacles. She wanted nothing more than to reach out and touch the permanently etched love of literature that encased his body. Finally, it was his grin that pulled her eyes back up to his lips. He'd done it on purpose; she was sure of it. Standing there, in a slight pose, allowing her the opportunity.

"No one's ever told me I snore. But if I do, just throw a pillow at me, and I'm sure I'll stop," he said.

Henley crawled into the bed. She melted a little as she took in the scent of books and the masculine smell of Garret, a mix of salty and sweet that tickled her nose. "Okay."

"Okay," he said and got to the floor, covering himself with the blankets, punching the pillow and settling.

From where she was lying, she had the perfect view of him. She peered over the mattress and looked down at Garret, his eyes already closed, breathing steadily. He had the most kissable-looking lips...

That was the last thing Henley thought about before letting the exhaustion and frustration of the day consume her.

* * *

When Henley woke, she had an uncomfortable second of unfamiliar surroundings. It took her a moment to adjust, but she was pleasantly surprised by how well she'd slept, and smiled at Garret's thoughtfulness from the instant he'd met her. But when she looked at the floor, the makeshift bed was rumpled and empty. It was then she saw a pad of paper and pen laying on top of his pillow. Henley looked around; the bathroom door hung open and unoccupied. He'd gotten up and left her alone. Curious, though, she slid from the bed and picked up the notepad.

You sleep like the dead. AND snore. Don't worry. It's cute. Fresh coffee and muffins downstairs when you're ready. But first... I want 150 creative words about coffee. GO!

Henley laughed and hugged the pad to her chest as she walked back to the bed and got under the covers. She lay still for a few minutes, but then she took the pen and started writing. It wasn't much. One hundred and fifty words was about a page. Less even. And coffee was an easy subject to write about. She'd worked in a café, after all. She felt the familiar tingling as an idea began to form and take hold. She wrote the words from the coffee's point of view, how it must feel starting out as a bean, being taken away from his family only to be tortured and ground up. Then forced to mix with water—its enemy—infected by the liquid and turned into coffee. Before Henley knew it, she'd written far more than the demanded one hundred and fifty words, and she hadn't felt so good about something in a long while. She knew, had her father been there to read it, he'd have loved the short tale and tragic life of coffee.

After changing back into the shorts and t-shirt she'd worn before, she ran her hands through her tangled blonde hair. Next, she bounded down the stairs—well, tried to gracefully bound, letting the thrill of writing carry her to the bookstore.

Henley found Garret behind the counter; he'd been mid-swallow, pulling a paper coffee cup from his lips. She couldn't contain her excited smile.

"Where's the coffee?" she said.

He held up a cup, but then wiggled the fingers of his other hand. "Let me see," he said in reference to the pad she still had in hand.

"What? No."

"Sorry, Henley, I can't give you the coffee until I know you've done your homework." Reluctantly she held out the pad of paper and took the coffee from Garret, taking an immediate sip, letting the warmth rush down her throat. When she came to his side, she saw four paper coffee cups lined up under the ledge of counter.

"Addicted much?"

Garret glanced down and had she not been looking right at him; she might have missed the slight rosiness that crept over his cheeks. "I promised fresh coffee. Then I didn't know when you'd wake up. So... I... just kept going next store and getting a new one."

Touched. The insane gesture completely and utterly moved Henley. The butterflies in her stomach reacted forcefully, and her heart skittered in her chest. "You didn't have to."

"I wanted to." Then he looked down at the paper and began to read. He was silent for a second. Then he laughed and smiled. When he finished, he looked at

Henley with an adoring gaze. "Brilliant. See, you are a writer. No mistaking it."

Henley waved him off. "One silly story about coffee does not a writer make."

"Maybe not. But it's a start." He reached into a bag and pulled out a muffin. "It's chocolate chip. I figured that was the safe choice."

"It was the perfect choice." Henley held the muffin as a bit of sadness took over the moment. She should be heading back home now. She'd probably overstayed her welcome, and yet, as Garret messed with a few of the books on the counter, she wondered, again, what it would be like to feel his lips against hers. To have his strong arms wrapped around her waist in a comforting embrace. And she wondered, did he smell as good as the sheets she'd cozied up in? "Can I stay?" She blurted out before her brain had a chance to censor her thoughts.

Garret looked up at her and without hesitation replied, a little hoarse in tone, "As long as you want."

They shared an instant connection that crackled between them. Sparks igniting the blood in Henley's veins and warmth spreading through her. Even if she didn't get the chance to experience his kisses or his tender touch, it wouldn't matter. Right then, Henley was sure that where she needed to be was with him. He could give her something far better than the hopes of getting her book back. She'd felt the inkling of a whispering muse as she wrote and was eager to see if she could coax the voice to come out even more. Henley owed it to herself to at least try, and because she was less than eager about making the journey home, and had nothing to go back to yet, it was the best option. The only one that made sense to her.

"But I might suggest a trip to the store. I can come with you if you want. I just don't have any of those girly things you might need. And you looked good in my sweats, but I doubt you want to walk around in those. And I don't have food. Like, at all," he rambled, looking nervous.

"I think you're right. That sounds like a good idea."

Henley headed towards the door and pushed it open. Garret came to her side, and once they were on the concrete walk, without warning, he scooped her hand into his. He looked over at her, smiled and gave it a reassuring squeeze. Just the slightest touch from him and the gaze of his eyes on her had Henley beginning to unravel with desire.

* * *

When they got back to the bookstore, Henley unloaded the few things she bought in the apartment while Garret went back to work. She took the time to shower, shave her legs, brush her teeth and change into a clean dress she'd bought at one of the shops in town. She thought back to Garret waiting outside the change room while she quickly tossed on the dresses she'd brought in. Henley had told Garret he could wait outside, or head back to the bookstore—she could find her way back, but he insisted on staying by her side the whole time. She was quick, made a few purchases, helped him buy a few groceries and headed back. The whole time he grasped her hand tightly, and she loved how it had made her feel. He was attentive, and she had begun to realize quickly that it was going to be hard for her to leave when the time came.

"I've got to unload these boxes that just came in. You can hang out here, or upstairs. Whatever you'd like," Garret said.

"I can hang out here." She tilted her chin towards the chair she'd sat in yesterday. "But I wonder... could you give me something to write about?"

He smiled. "I thought you'd never ask. Okay, let me think—" He rubbed his hand over his chin. "How about five hundred words about this place. The bookstore."

"Okay. I can do that. I think."

"Of course you can. Just don't give up."

Henley felt a pang in her heart at his words. They stung her eyes, and she was propelled back to a memory with her father. He'd done the same thing. Giving her little ideas about what to write about, urging her just to let the words come without thinking too hard about it. It didn't matter if what you wrote wasn't good, it just mattered that you had the courage to write in the first place.

"Did I say something wrong?" Concerned filled his tone, and his lips dipped in a frown.

"No. Not at all. It's just... never mind." She couldn't tell him about her father. She wasn't ready. "You're right. I can do it."

"Good. Now get to it, young lady." He tried to sound stern, keep a straight face, but he broke out in a broad grin.

Henley curled up in the chair, paper and pen in hand. She closed her eyes and waited, hoped the whisper of her muse would come to her, tickling her insides with an idea. She counted silently to ten, inhaling deep calming breaths, and then she heard something, but it wasn't the voice she'd expected. It sounded an awful lot like Garret's. She smirked as she looked over the pages, leaning a little to the left in the chair, just to get a better view of him. He lugged a few boxes out from the backroom. Henley wondered where he'd possibly find the space for them.

She began to write a few minutes later. About a worm. It was silly, but he'd felt lost, different, and the other worms made fun of him because he needed glasses to see, and loved to read. But then, when he was out trying to find something from the street to read, it began to rain and he got lost. He saw the glow of the store, Re: Read Books, and snuck inside. He was enamored by the amount of reading there for him to absorb himself in. He no longer felt lost, instead, feeling right at home. He stayed there forever.

It was a silly story, but Henley had a gleam in her eye when she finished. She yawned and stretched.

"Do I get to read it?"

"No. I don't think so," she teased, clutching the pad tightly in her hands.

Garret frowned and took a few calculated steps towards Henley. "But you looked like you had written something fantastic. I could almost feel the inspiration emanating from you."

"Maybe if you give me another prompt, you can."

"Or..." Garret pounced on her and started tickling Henley, his fingers dancing over her hips. She cried with laughter, trying to push him away while not giving up the paper. But she lost the battle. He ended up with the story when he'd stopped, their faces inches away from each other. She could see hunger in his eyes as he looked at her lips. Henley swallowed thickly. She'd been right. He smelled just as delicious as his bed, and it wrapped around her, tingling in places she would never have expected. Between the look, the smell, and how one of his hands still rested on her bare knee, Henley was charmed by his presence.

"I might kiss you," he said.

"I might want you to."

Slowly, Garret inched towards her. He slid his hand from her knee, up her side, over her arm, and settled it on her neck, his thumb brushing across her lips. Naturally, she licked them with her tongue in anticipation. Time slowed down for Henley when he closed the distance and placed his lips against hers. At first, it was just a tender touch. A delicate movement of their lips against each other's, but then he tilted her head up, deepening the motion, taking her bottom lip into his mouth, teasing it with his teeth.

The world slipped away as they kissed. Melting into each other. Desperate to release a passion that awakened Henley in a glorious way. Her thoughts began to shift from not knowing what it was like to have his lips upon her and his hands against her skin, to wanting more. She barely knew him, but he didn't feel like a stranger, at all. It was as though her lips knew his. That his hands were reconnecting with a body they recognized. The ease of the lust that consumed them made it seem like they were just finding their way home.

At the sound of the door, Garret pulled back, shattering the perfection of their kiss. She missed it instantly, longing to feel it again.

"Hey, Mrs. Graham." Garret stood, and took a few steps towards her. "What can I help you with?"

Mrs. Graham smiled knowingly, and when Garret wasn't looking, she winked at Henley. "I'm just looking for something. I can come back though if you're otherwise indisposed."

Garret coughed and straightened out his shirt, adjusting his jeans. "Nope. I'm good. Just give me a second." He walked back to Henley and kneeled down, placing his hands on her knees. He gave them a squeeze, and she bit her lip, nervously. He whispered, just loud enough for her to hear, "I want you to write about what you're thinking, right now. How you're feeling. And how much you want me." He moved his hands from her legs, placing them on the arms of the chair, and as he got up, he stopped right in front of Henley, leveling his gaze with hers. He lingered for all of ten seconds before he leaned the rest of the way in and seized Henley's lips again. She melted. The ache she felt all over increased in intensity, turning her on in a way that unexpectedly gained dominance over everything else.

"Alright, Mrs. Graham, what can I help you find?" The two disappeared into the maze of books while Henley was left gasping for air.

When Henley calmed herself down, and was able to ignore the tingle that had spread over her body, she began to write. It was easy. She was more than lusting for Garret, and she allowed his voice to become her muse, guiding her forward. There was a sense of delving into the unknown. She'd never written about herself in such a way, nor put to light the desires that had begun to well within her. But she did what she could, turning it into a semi-work of fiction. Though she and Garret were the main characters, the situations she put them in were very different. After Mrs. Graham had left the store, occasionally Henley would glance up from the page to find Garret looking at her. She blushed, and went right back to writing.

Before long Henley had filled dozens of pages with her less than neat scrawl, and Garret was flipping the sign on the door over to "closed," ending his work day.

"Aren't you done yet?" He came to her side and kissed her cheek, trying to steal a peek at the story Henley was writing.

"Nope."

"I can't believe just yesterday you weren't calling yourself a writer, told me you'd lost it. Looks to me like you've had no trouble finding the voice again."

Henley looked up at him. "I'm not sure I've found the voice completely, but I've come across something worth writing about."

"Well, that's a start, and I'm glad I've been able to help."

It occurred to Henley that she hadn't thanked him for what he'd done. He'd taken her in, given her shelter, and showed her she still could write. That the creativity inside her wasn't lost. It just... needed to be found again. Though she wasn't overwhelmed with a million novel ideas, she had one. And that was better than nothing.

"Thank you. For everything. I-I don't—"

"Hey, don't worry about it. Besides, don't thank me yet. You haven't tried my cooking. You might regret ever meeting me."

Henley was sure that would be impossible. From what she'd been through over the last day and a half, she couldn't imagine how she'd gone through life without knowing him. He had managed to wiggle into her heart, abruptly, and was slowly righting her world.

While Garret cooked, Henley wrote. She lay on his bed and let her pen feverishly scribble across the pages. It was only supposed to be a short story, a few pages at most, but Henley couldn't control herself, or the words that spilled onto the lined pad. She also didn't want to stop, for fear she'd lose Garret's whisper from inside her.

"Okay. I'm ready. Now I warn you... I've been a bachelor for a lot of years... I don't generally cook for two."

She moved from the bed and to the table. "I'm sure it'll be great, whatever it is." Henley looked down at the plate set in front of her. "What is it?" she teased. Garret went in for a tickling. Now that he'd discovered she giggled uncontrollably, he did it often. "Okay, okay. I give up. I'm kidding. It's steak. And potatoes, with asparagus. And some brown goo." She couldn't resist.

"It's peppercorn gravy. Makes everything taste better."

"If you say so." She cut into her steak and took a bite. There was an explosion of flavors that hit her tongue. He'd been modest. He was an amazing cook, and everything was delicious.

"I don't want to pry, but... I'm wondering, now that you know me a little better, and slept in my bed, if you'd tell me about yesterday. About you. Your life."

Henley became rigid as she set down her fork. She'd spent the better part of the day blissfully ignoring the life she'd left behind. It was like she'd stepped into her own novel, a work of fiction that she still, at times, wondered if it was real. Or if she was still lying in the hospital, dreaming. But deep down, she knew it was real because although it pained her to do so, she'd sent Abigail a text, just to tell her she was fine. She ignored how she'd felt when she checked her phone to find a dozen messages and a flurry of texts. Even if she didn't want to, she cared—a little—about what her mother was going through, sick with worry.

"Things just got out of control. I was in a car accident a while back, and it changed me. Not just on the out-side." She looked down at her leg, rubbing the dull ache that was ever present. "And I lost something very dear to me that day, and I've been trying to get a piece of it back."

"The Write Way."

"Yes. It was a gift from my dad before he died. I kept it with me, always. I honestly did believe that the book and he were the muses in my soul. I wanted to be a writer. An author. But after the accident and the loss of the book, I-I guess I gave up."

"I'm sorry. I am. But giving up is okay. You went through something... tragic. And it's understandable, but you can't, you can never let those things change you, especially not for the worse. Part of being a writer is working through the blocks you create in your mind."

"I'm figuring that out, now, thanks to you."

"Well, I'm glad I was here when you needed some-one." Then he said, "So, can I read your story yet?"

She smiled bashfully. "Nope. It's not done."

He sighed. "Okay."

* * *

After helping Garret clear the dishes, staying up a lit-tle longer to talk, and getting to know more about him,

Henley changed into his sweats and t-shirt from the night before. She sat on his bed and kept writing, while he lay on the floor, reading.

"I can't take it anymore. This is your bed. It's big enough for the two of us."

Garret set the book on his stomach, tilting his head towards her. "Yes, but I'm a gentleman."

"And I'm giving you permission."

He didn't have to be told twice. He lifted himself from the floor and sat down on the bed, Henley scooching over to give him room. They rested, at first, against the wall, shoulder to shoulder, but as Henley kept writing, she found herself leaning into him. He lifted up his arm and wrapped it around her, pulling her against him. She fit. Perfectly. Securely. She found her writing slowed, as she became more aware of how close they were. How her heart lurched towards him. How her mind had begun to wander from the words she'd been writing, the fantasies she was creating, to reality, and wanted to make those scenes come alive.

"Are you done?" He looked away from the book he was reading.

"No." But she couldn't concentrate, not on the story. Henley was paying more attention to how she took two breaths to Garret's one. That his eyes twitched when he neared the end of the page he was reading. Or that he turned the top, rather than the bottom. And when he looked over at her, all she could think about was wanting to feel his lips on hers again. Even the tattoos captivated her, drawn to their beauty, they were like nothing she'd ever seen before.

"Okay. I'm saying you're done. For now." He grabbed the paper and tossed it in the air. It landed with a thud.

"Hey, don't you want to read it?"

Garret laughed, and she felt it shiver up her spine. "It's been awhile, Henley, but I'm pretty sure I still remember how to pleasure a woman. I don't need a story to give me ideas. If you'll let me try?" He dropped his book onto the floor and in the next second was kissing her, never giving her a chance to respond or catch her breath.

The way she kissed him back, gripping him tightly, was answer enough. Garret's tongue swept over her bottom lip, seeking entrance, and Henley was all too willing to give it to him, parting her lips with a sigh. He tasted of the strong black coffee he'd drank after dinner, mixed with mouthwash. His hand rested on her stomach, searing her with his hot touch. Urging the kiss, the mingling of their tongues, to deepen even further as he slid his hand over to her hip, lowering her into the plush pillows, gaining more access to her.

The barrier of clothes between them was more than Henley could handle. She desperately wanted to shed them in order to connect even more with him. Garret had already taken off his shirt and was wearing only boxers, but in the heat of the moment, it was still too much. She let her hands find his bare skin, smoothing them over his back, down his hips and up the front of his chest. He returned the motion, using his hands to explore Henley.

He slipped one hand, slowly, underneath her shirt. She'd already taken off the bra she'd been wearing earlier when she'd changed.

The anticipation of his hand sliding up her stomach towards her breasts caused her nipples to tighten, and a wonderful sensation to tingle between her legs. When he suddenly stopped, she tried to hold the disappointment inside.

"Is this okay? I mean, I want to—"

"Yes. I want to," she breathed.

When his hand cupped her breast, she unintentionally gasped, pushing into him. Garret pulled back, but when he saw the look in her eyes, he knew he didn't need to stop. He delicately pinched her nipple, and then moved his hand to her other breast and did the same.

"Can we lose the shirt?" he asked, but added, "I don't want to push you too far, too fast but..." He slid even closer to her, his erection apparent through his boxers. He was allowing her to feel how aroused he was. How much he wanted her. "I'm afraid I'm not sure I'll be able to stop if you do, so be warned," he said, tone rough.

In answer, she grasped the fabric of her shirt and slid it over her head. "I don't want you to stop."

Garret inhaled a ragged breath at the sight of her completely visible to him. She had a few scars from the accident, from the shattered glass of the windows. Henley thought she might have been self-conscious about the marks. They speckled her torso and chest. There were a few on her arm and legs, but she'd gotten used to those quicker. But as Garret kissed each one, tenderly, she didn't care. They were a part of who she was, and he didn't seem to mind the look of them at all. His actions were slow and deliberate, working his way back up, until his tongue was sweeping over her, his teeth teasing her nipple, sending a wave of lust to warm her core. She felt it all over, a tremble, as goose-bumps prickled her skin.

"How did I get so lucky?" he said, but didn't give Henley a chance to respond. His mouth found hers again, crushing their lips together.

He moved slightly, resting a little bit more of his weight on her. He was warm, toned, and Henley relished in the feel of his skin pressed against hers, the heat between them flaring up even hotter. She was slowly growing more desperate to have him. All of him. But he was taking his time, enjoying the moment, the connection, pleasuring her. But when his hand dipped underneath the sweat pants she was wearing, Henley didn't think she could handle much more. The pressure building was becoming almost painful, yet enticing. She couldn't remember the last time she'd been consumed entirely with desire and was eager to have it shatter her.

Garret was sensual with his touch when he reached down. He pushed her legs farther apart, giving him more access, and then in one swift motion, he moved his hand over her. She arched her back, desperate for more. Then he glided his finger between the delicate folds of her core, glistening with wetness, ready for his touch. She inhaled sharply as he began to stroke her affectionately. Concentrating at first on moving his finger over her increasingly swollen clit, he rubbed circles around it, then dipped his finger inside, only to slip out the next second. He teased her mercilessly, until she writhed beneath his touch, her hips working in slow circles, heightening the movements of his hand.

When she was near the brink, coming undone, Garret covered her breast with his other hand, rolling her taut nipple between his fingers. Henley bit down on her lip, her eyes pinching shut as she breathed deeply. The concentration of his fingers, in all the right places, sent a tidal wave of sensitivity to shudder through her. She convulsed, her core exploding with wetness as he drew his finger inside her again, working her with a little more force than before, helping her ride out the orgasm that had grabbed hold of her.

But he didn't stop, not right away. Henley was still coming down, and Garret was already working her up again by engaging her further. He pulled the pants over her hips. She helped him by shimmying her body until they landed on the floor.

Garret lifted himself until he was hovering over her dampened body. His eyes swept over her and down to her newly uncovered skin. Henley was completely bare to him, and she couldn't help but drown in the hungry expression of his eyes. Henley expected him to slide his boxers down and reveal himself to her. She was ready. More than ready. But what he did next was move farther down the length of her body and press his lips against the inside of both of her thighs. The electricity that quivered over her was tantalizing, and when Garret parted her and gave her one long and hard stroke of his tongue, the burning ache was building up again, becoming more incessant and intense.

"You taste so sweet," he said, then licked her throbbing clit again. He applied just the right amount of pressure and sucked, lapping up her wetness.

Henley moaned with pleasure as he began a succession of rhythmic movements, tongue over her tender flesh, then pushing against her entrance. She trembled. He hadn't been lying. He certainly knew all the right moves to pleasure her. She was slick with sweat, full of an almost unbearable amount of arousal, and anxious for the onslaught of another devastating orgasm. Her hands fisted the sheets as she drew closer to coming. He lifted her up, resting his hand on her backside, pressing himself against her more, sweeping over her with more force, until she had no choice but to let go. He gripped her tightly, working his tongue, and sucking with his lips, coaxing her over the edge. She came with an irresistible force she hadn't expected. It sent waves of awareness to spark her nerves with almost blinding desire.

"Mmm. That was..." Henley began, trying to find her voice.

"Amazing," he finished for her.

Peacefully, with hooded eyes, she replied, "Yes. Definitely." She licked her lips.

"If you'll just give me a minute, I'd like to see if we can do better..."

Henley didn't think that were possible, but she nodded with an eager grin. Garret went into the bathroom, and from the bed Henley heard him fight to get the box of condoms open he had stashed in the medicine cabinet.

He reappeared a minute later, holding the square foiled wrapper. When he reached the side of the bed, he pulled down his boxers. He was absolutely ready for more, his erection standing tall. Garret pulled the package open, but Henley was quick to take it from him. He'd been in control thus far, but she courageously wanted to take it from him.

"Come here. Closer," she said, beckoning him with a wiggle of her fingers. He was quick to action, and Henley sat up, taking him into her hand. She gave his hardness a few strokes, Garret groaning at her movements. She worked him harder but stopped to put the condom over his tip and unroll it down his length. Before she could lose the courage she'd mustered up, she said, "Would you lie down?" She winked and shot him a daring look.

Henley shuffled over, giving him room. She had gathered the sheets of the bed around her when Garret had gotten up, but quickly discarded them and climbed over him. She guided his erection, allowing her to slide over his length easily. Henley was slow, letting herself relax, yet clenching around his cock until she'd lowered herself all the way down. She wiggled her hips, teasing him, only to lean forward and capture Garret's lips, smoothing her hands over his tousled brown hair. He wrapped his arms around her, tightly, but then slid them down to her backside, forcing her to move against him. She let Garret control her speed, sliding up and down, working her hips, until she could no longer keep up and pulled her mouth from him with a moan of pleasure.

Henley took his hands into hers, pulling them up, placing them over her breasts as she rolled her hips. He squeezed and pinched her nipples, provoking a whimper as his hands moved over her skin. She felt the buildup deep within her, starting out as another dull ache, but progressing quickly. Henley worked her hips harder, pushing into him, expanding the connection they shared. When she felt herself reaching closer to another climax, she leaned further back, sliding up and down his length, driving herself into him as deeply as she could.

It wasn't quite enough, and with Garret's hands still on her breasts, she reached down and eagerly slipped her fingers over her engorged clitoris, helping herself along. Garret's eyes grew wide, and a crooked grin stretched over his mouth. She smiled proudly at how undone he was becoming when he groaned, lifting up his head to watch her pleasure herself, her hips still working against him.

Garret tensed first, his hands falling from her chest onto her thighs as he grunted, pinching his eyes closed. Henley worked her fingers faster, knowing he wouldn't be able to hold on much longer, and ground into him with all the force she could handle. Her breathing became ragged as she felt her core tighten around Garret, as she gave her swollen clit a few more delicate strokes,

just enough to push her over the edge. She came quickly, her entire body clenching and shuddering as she
worked to keep up her speed so they could both ride out
their climax together.

When Henley finally stilled, she was met with the
most alluring gaze coming from Garret, and it sent one
last tremor to take control of her body, one more lingering sensation that she delighted in.

She climbed off and lay down beside him, resting her
head on Garret's chest. His heart ran rapid, and his
breathing had only now begun to ease. Henley, herself,
was out of breath, still tingling with sensations that ignited her body with a glorious flash of heat and coolness.

"I just need a minute, okay?" Garret's voice cut
through the silence. And when she nodded against his
chest, he got up from the bed.

Henley had never felt more satisfied in her life, yet
was utterly exhausted. When Garret came back, she let
him wrap around her, holding her close. He kissed her
lips, her temple and then whispered, "I wish I could keep
you, forever."

Her heart broke a little, knowing she couldn't stay.
That she had to go back and at the very least, deal with
the shitstorm that was waiting for her.

A few minutes later, Garret had drifted into a deep
slumber, his own exhaustion taking over. But Henley
couldn't still her mind. She knew she should be tired.
That what they had just done should have worn her out.
At first, she simply mapped out his tattoos, fingers dancing along the curve of his torso. She read the famous

quotes, the lines of literature, was mesmerized by the dedication he had and his proud display of his love of books. Eventually, though, Henley found herself slipping from the bed, only to gather up the pad of paper that was discarded earlier. The voice within was persistent, loud, and she wanted to finish the story she'd begun earlier. It was an odd feeling, having her muse come out, willing to thrust ideas upon her. She accepted it, not knowing if it would truly last.

* * *

The morning came too quickly for Henley. When her eyes opened, Garret was already awake, his fingers skimming across the skin of her back.

"Good morning, beautiful," he said, leaning in for a kiss. "What should we do today? The store's closed on Sundays, so you have me all to yourself if you want."

Henley wanted nothing more than to spend the day with him. She did, but she knew she couldn't. "I have to go back."

Rolling over, Garret let out a huff. "When?"

The burn of salty tears was quick to fill Henley's eyes. "Now. I just think—I have so much to deal with. I can't stay here, even though I want to."

Solemnly, he said, "I know. But does it have to be now?"

"I think it would make it easier, so yeah, it has to be now." She tore herself away from him, even though it hurt her heart. "There's just so much going on right now.

I need time to sort it out." She got up from the bed and gathered up her clothes. Henley couldn't look at Garret; tried to look anywhere else. She knew, if she did, she'd want to climb right back into his arms and hide forever.

"Okay, well just give me a minute and I'll go next door and grab us a coffee. Stay for breakfast, at least."

It was only delaying the inevitable, but she couldn't say no. "Alright. I can do that."

He was quick to get up and yank on his clothes. "Chocolate chip muffin?"

"Yes, please. And a big, tall cup of black coffee."

"Of course, it's the only way to drink it." He smiled, but it didn't quite reach his eyes. They were missing the twinkle she'd seen in them last night.

When Garret left the apartment, Henley gathered up the rest of her stuff. She tore out the countless pages of the story she'd spent the remainder of the night writing. Henley had planned to take it with her, but then thought he might like to read it. It was, after all, written for him. She was quick to look through the drawers in the kitchen and found a box of envelopes wedged between rolls of duct tape and various tools. She pulled one from the box and shoved the papers inside, sealing it. She half expected the voice to be trapped inside the envelope but when she closed her eyes and listened, it was still there. Henley had managed to find the voice inside her, brought it out, and she didn't need the book or the memory of her father to do it. What she needed was a chance just to get away and be herself, be happy. She wasn't filled with the overload of ideas like before, but she knew all she needed was one. To find one thing to write about and go from there.

Henley was standing in the middle of the apartment when Garret came back, juggling two cups of coffee and paper bag filled with muffins. "Are you all packed up?" He saw her stuff covering the table. "Oh, here, let me get you a bag for that." Garret passed her a cup of coffee and dropped the rest on the counter. He headed over to the linen closet and pulled out a well-used backpack and brought it back to her.

Once she was done shoving it full with her few belongings, Garret said, "Did you get everything out of the bathroom? You should probably double check." The sadness in his tone was evident as he put on a fake smile, adding, "I don't have much use for girly shampoo." He rubbed his hands over his head and forced a smile.

Though she was sure she'd gotten everything, Henley went to look, just in case. It didn't matter much, but realized that maybe it would be painful for him if she'd left any trace of herself behind. She thought about the envelope she'd shoved between the pages of the book he'd been reading. He'd have to deal with that.

"Yeah, I got everything." She added, "I should really hit the road," when she was standing in front of Garret.

"I put an extra muffin in the bag." Then he said, looking down at the floor, "This is hard. I didn't think it would be this hard." He reached for her, pulling Henley into a hug. "I don't want to be just a one-night stand that you forget about. I want more if you'll give it to me. I'll wait. I'll be here."

Henley brushed at the tears that threatened to fall. "I want more too. I'm just not ready."

"I know. It's okay. Really. I'm just glad that you came here and managed to put some of the pieces of your life back together. And that I helped you, a little, with reconnecting with your muse. You're a great writer. You'll make a brilliant author, I know it."

He was talking like he'd never see her again, and Henley knew, maybe that was for the better. Her life had suddenly laid out two very different paths for her, having brought Garret to her. She had to figure out if she could cross them and make them work together. She wanted to finish college. Henley wanted to be an author. And she wanted, more than anything in the world to be with Garret.

"Thank you. For everything." She pulled back and placed her hands on his cheeks, and leaned in for one last tender kiss. It didn't feel like enough. But all Henley could give Garret was one last fleeting moment, and when she pulled away, she scooped up the backpack from the table, and headed for the door.

"Just remember, don't give up."

She didn't look back. Couldn't. It hurt too much. Henley hated how she'd fallen for someone who had been a stranger not more than two days before. Typically, she kept her heart guarded, but Garret could have had all of her if she'd been weaker.

164

The ride home was excruciating. Henley took it slow, stretching it out as long as she could. She made a few stops, stretched her legs, and enjoyed the scenery she missed on the way down. Somewhere in the middle, Henley's stomach growled, and she'd remembered what Garret had said about the extra muffin he'd stashed in her bag. When she pulled the zipper, she was surprised to find something in there she didn't recognize. Her hand grabbed the foreign object and yanked it out. Henley turned the wrapped rectangle in her fingers. It couldn't be...

She ripped off the paper to reveal a worn copy of The Write Way. She clutched it to her chest as emotions overwhelmed her. Henley then flipped it open the cover, to the first page. A square piece of paper fluttered to the ground, but she was more interested in the messy blue scrawl. Her thumb ran over the indentations of the words her father had written so long ago. She began to cry, blinking her eyes over and over at the impossibility of the book she now held in her hands. She worried that it wasn't real.

I wouldn't have ever believed in fate, if not for this book. I'm sorry I didn't have the courage to give it to you right away. But it seems you were meant to find it. And I hope that means you were meant to find me, too. That together, we brought the muse back into your life.

It took every inch of Henley's will not to pull her car around and speed back to Garret. She wanted to. Badly. But if the book was proof, and it found its way back to her, that meant she'd find her way back to him, when she was ready. One perfect weekend wouldn't make up for all the wrong in her life. She needed to have the strength to follow her dreams, on her terms. And she needed to put the pieces of her heart back together before she would ever be able to give it to someone completely. She'd been in search of her muse. Running away when life got hard. But what Henley discovered was the voice had never truly left, she'd just lost sight of what she wanted.

She wouldn't make that mistake again.

Beneath the Inhibitions

THE FORT made of partially soiled black table linens, dusty-rose colored high back chairs, and tables, smelled of sweet hazelnuts. The distinct aroma came from an open bottle of Frangelico, mixing with the warmth and sweat of several authors hidden beneath the canopy. A tune from an iPod swirled around the conversation, going mostly unnoticed.

Piper's eyes adjusted to the dim light that glowed from the screen. Having just been on the outside, she timidly reclaimed her spot. It was a small patch of carpet, dampened with the remnants of spilled beer. She looked around at the shadowed faces before her. Some she knew, but most she didn't. Unexpectedly, Piper wondered how she'd found herself with a warming can of beer in her hands and a name on the tip of her tongue.

Right, she reminded herself. She'd been asked to send someone named Gavin a message. That had probably been the only reason she'd re-entered the makeshift fort, at the epicenter of another raging night at Northern Write Con. Piper wasn't one to disappoint. Besides, interest intrigued her. Who was this Gavin, and how was it that she'd spent the better part of the night without knowing who she was rubbing elbows with?

Apparently, he gave good hugs, too, which only heightened her desire to meet him.

Draining the last of her beer, she swiped an arm across her dry lips, swallowing down, for a second, her shyness.

In a tone that came out more question than confident, she asked, "Is there a Gavin in here?"

The titter of several conversations muted, dark eyes suddenly shifted to Piper. Moisture began to form on her brow. Jitters in her hands caused her to clench them tight in her lap, as her heart jerked and picked up pace.

Never more than in that moment had she felt so out of place. An unknown and inexperienced author sticking out in the crowd like a bad cliché nestled in between profound prose.

She was still relatively new; barely what you'd considered up and coming, like some of the other names that jumped off the pages of the weekend program. The green around her edges showed as someone across the fort giggled, just as a voice, laced with laughter, spoke out from beside her.

"That's me. I'm Gavin."

Piper's body became rigid as she tilted her head to the right. She could have sworn the spot beside her was unoccupied. Her composure was slow to return, as she formed a string of words together that wouldn't make her stand even more apart from everyone else.

"Ah. Gavin," she started. "I come bearing news from the outside."

She held still, the words rolling over him, as the outline of a grin stretched across his face.

Something about that barely visible smile allowed her to relax a little.

"And what news do you bring, milady?" he asked in character, coming from a man of authority and wealth. A silly plot they'd begun to work out earlier, of a fort, kings and queens, and the outsiders, lowly commoners.

"I've been told to tell you, you owe someone a hug." Piper silently cursed, having forgotten the author's name that had asked her to pass along the message. She'd met dozens of people over the course of the last two days. Too many names to remember.

Gavin seemed to sense this. He made a gesture as he asked, "Was she short?"

Piper nodded, biting her lower lip.

He chuckled, which sent a shiver up Piper's spine and down to her toes that were tucked into a clean pair of sneakers. The sensation tickled her stomach in a way that caused more nervous sweat to seep from her pores.

"I mentioned in one of my workshops that I was a hugger," he said as if answer enough for the odd messaged she'd just relayed.

At his remark, Piper's eyes drifted closed as she recalled the names of the honored guests of the weekend. One, in particular, came crashing forward.

"You're Gavin from..." her voice lowered to a whisper, but apparently loud enough for him to hear.

"I am," he replied with confidence.

If it had been socially acceptable and wouldn't have raised eyebrows, Piper would have smacked herself. Here, for the better part of the night, she'd been sitting, legs and arms touching, next to one of the most influential people at the conference. A bookseller by trade, from one of the few well-known companies in America. Seemed he moonlighted as an author, too, having published several works of both fiction and non, from what she'd read of his bio tucked right at the front of the program.

Shifting her body, she held out a shaky hand toward him. It hung in the air for second, untouched, as Piper swallowed, saying, "I'm Piper," introducing herself to the publishing magnate.

Then, smoothly, he glided his fingers over her skin and shook her hand firmly. Warmth crept over her cheeks as Piper debated what to say next. "We should be friends," came out before she could censor herself.

"You do, do you?" He chuckled.

She nodded. It was then, with his hand still held with hers, the glow from the iPod managed to expose him a little more to her. He wore a tailored black jacket, over top of a black button-up shirt. At first, what caught her attention was the stark contrast of the pop of white from the tie slung around his neck.

Boldly, Piper released his hand, instantly feeling the loss of contact, only to reach toward him. The silky tie, adorned with skulls, glided through her fingertips. Her eyebrows raised in question. It was a slightly odd sight since it wasn't Halloween. He was dressed in clothes for an entirely different occasion than everyone else. Most wore jeans and T-shirts, summer dresses, and sandals. Piper self-consciously looked down at her simple Capri length jeans, yellow and black blouse, and her sneakers, as the last of the tie slipped over her skin.

Gavin plucked the fabric up and said, "I like to dress up for these things," inspecting the tie with a scrutinizing expression.

"Apparently, I don't." She motioned to the tie, now resting against his chest. "I actually have one just like it," Piper replied quickly. She thought back to her closet, a hanger filled with ties of all colors and patterns, tucked away with an array of clothes for all occasions. For the conference, she had only brought the bare minimum. Had she known people would dress up, she might have packed differently.

"You have a men's tie?"

"It was a phase." Piper shrugged. "I wore them before Avril Lavigne made it cool."

He nodded in answer. Piper cast her gaze downward, wondering if that was a silly thing to say to a guy like Gavin.

Silence settle between them as Piper struggled for something to say to uncover the uncomfortable cloak that had drawn around them. "Do you have a card?"

"I do," he replied, coolly. Gavin pulled open his jacket, plunging his hand into the breast pocket. He pulled out a crisp business card and passed it over.

Their fingers brushed as Piper took the stiff cardstock from his hand, a zip of electricity coming with the brief exchange. She clutched it, as yet again, she struggled to find her voice. He had an odd effect on her tongue, tying it in knots.

"Are you a writer?" he asked, pulling Piper's gaze back to his obscured features.

She cleared her throat as she shoved the card into her back pocket. "Author. I have two books published," she replied, but a sinking feeling settled into the pit of her stomach, twisting it with unease.

Piper may have two published books to her name, but that was as far as her bibliography went. Her agent was trying to sell a third, but if she was honest with herself that might have been all the creative prose she had in her.

Somewhere, somehow, over the last while, she'd lost her nerve. Lost the ability to put pen to paper. Her muse, the creative being that lived in her soul and fuelled her with the ability to write, had disappeared. It was as though Piper had woken up one day, and everything thing was different.

The millions of ideas, the plots of stories yet to be written; the characters that usually formed in her mind and talked incessantly, were gone. Her mind was utterly silent, and the creativity well had dried up.

At first, Piper thought her muse had simply gone on vacation. It happened. She'd read about writers who had experienced something similar. But they always came back, the muse always found its way home. A good night's rest, a change of scenery, a different set of pace, Piper had tried it all, to no avail. It seemed, after almost a year, it was never going to burrow its way back into her soul.

"Well, you should email me, tell me about your books and maybe I can help get you some exposure."

Piper laughed to herself, on the inside, at the absurdity of the statement. She was a no-body, and he was a some-body. He was probably just saying it to be polite. Handing out the matte blue business card to everyone he met or asked for it. Maybe it made him feel better. Grabbing the hopes of struggling authors, raising them slightly, knowing that in some way, he held the power. He did. With a flick of his tie, in the right direction, he could probably do so much for an author. But Piper doubted that sort of attention came for free. Besides, she didn't need help with publicity, she needed her muse back to help her pen a bestseller.

* * *

As the party began to wrap up, Gavin having left the tent for more interesting conversation, Piper crawled from the canopy of table cloths. The harsh light was bright in her eyes as she stood, adjusted her top and stumbled toward the elevators.

A few people still milled about, half-empty glasses of amber liquor in their hands, as they struggled to stay upright. She waved to a few friendly faces as she passed by, but her steps slowed as a familiar rumble of laughter made way to her ears. Her attention perked as another strange wave of tingles fluttered in her stomach.

Her eyes danced around the occupied chairs and couches until she was able to find the source.

Gavin.

He was sitting with a few women, hands gesturing wildly.

Piper came to a stop, just as his eyes found hers. He nodded with a warm smile that grabbed her attention further, pulling it towards him, just as he reengaged in the conversation he was having.

In the brighter lights of the hallway, Piper was able to see Gavin for all he was.

Suddenly, and without warrant, Piper was mesmerized. The feeling odd as she took a hesitant step closer to him, her eyes sweeping up his length, starting at his polished black shoes, the slacks that covered long, lean legs; the jacket, button-up shirt and now undone tie. Piper took another step forward as she continued to appraise him.

Gavin looked older than she initially thought, than the tone his throaty laughter let on while they were inside the darkened fort. Instead of being put off by it, her attraction deepened. The nearly black hair salted with gray of his mustache goatee combo. There was a name for that, but it eluded her. Either way, it suited him well. It drew attention away from the hint of lines that creased his forehead and at the corners of his eyes; a shade of hazel, with flecks of green in them. They carried an intensity that Piper had never seen before. Yet, a gentleness that tugged at her heart.

His head was shaved to the quick, taking away from the severity of the receding hair line he might have had had he worn it longer. A harsh edge to him that went well with the softness of those eyes. Another feature that suited him well, she thought as she tried to picture a swath of longer, salt and pepper hair on him, but couldn't.

It was then that he cleared his throat, pulling her back to reality. A fresh wave of crimson spread over her cheeks at the realization he'd caught her staring.

With their eyes locked, Piper had to make a decision. She could drop her gaze to the floor and desperately try to escape. That didn't feel right. She couldn't reason with running away like a child. Instead, she closed the last bit of distance, almost joining the small circle of people, but yet, still an outsider. She swallowed thickly and said apprehensively, "I heard somewhere that you're a good hugger. I think you owe me one."

That was a little more direct than she had planned, but there was no turning back now.

Without hesitation, and a broad smile with gleaming white teeth, Gavin stood, motioning for her to come even closer.

Piper was suddenly swallowed up in his arms. Gavin was tall, and he dipped down slightly for a better hold. All too soon, however, he was pulling back. She wanted to grab hold of him, keep him pressed to her body, continuing to feel his strong muscles flex beneath his shirt.

Gavin stepped back, still grinning. "Did it live up to the expectation?" he asked.

Piper wanted nothing more than to have Gavin's arms around her again, the warmth that he exuded and the gentleness that comforted her, and he'd just given her an opening.

Though she feared for his ego, she shrugged nonchalantly. "It was alright. I mean, I've had better." Hoping he'd fall for the ruse and envelope her again.

A flicker of hurt pierced his gaze, pinching the lines of wrinkles at the corners, but another of his trademark smiles said the bruised ego was short lived. The frown lasted only a second and was gone in an instant. "I'm sorry." He frowned. "Maybe we should try it again. I really am a good hugger, I swear."

This time, Gavin pulled her close, even tighter than before. Piper inhaled deeply, her nostrils flaring at the tart scent of alcohol, sweat and aftershave that filled her nose. Her eyes fell closed as she pressed her head into his chest, gripping him just as tightly back; their bodies connecting in all the right places in an almost perfect fit. It was a safe feeling. Like she could have spent hours tucked within his grasp, feeling protected by his presence.

The embrace drew to a close. Though it had lasted twice as long, when he began to pull away, for Piper, it hadn't been nearly long enough. She swore she began to hear the barest of a whisper that tried to beckon her back towards him. By hug standards though, it broached scarcely on the scale of crossing between friendly and intimate. After all, they'd only just met, any longer would suggest otherwise to the now prying eyes of the group around them.

"There. Was that better? I really gave it my all."

It was perfect. Maybe the best hug of her life, she wanted to say but didn't. "That was a great hug."

He seemed satisfied with her answer, settling into his seat on the couch. Piper stood for an awkward second before turning on her heels, leaving Gavin to his friends. She headed the rest of the way towards the elevator, ready to call it a night.

* * *

Once she got to her hotel room, Piper was no longer tired. Something about the evening's events continued to rattle her. Something about Gavin further grabbed her attention. The attraction she felt still warming her insides.

She pulled her laptop from her bag and tossed it onto the bed. Next, she kicked off her shoes, stripped away the day's garments and replaced them with silky shorts and a sports bra. She washed away the makeup still caked on her face, then propped a few pillows up on the bed.

Settled against down-filled pillows, Piper opened the lid on the computer and connected to the internet. She told herself she would only look at Gavin's profile for a moment. When she Googled his name, she was surprised by how many results popped up. She clicked the top one, his website, and began to read with rapt interest.

A few moments later, she backed out, clicked on the next link, and kept reading, inhaling as much information as she could. If she saw Gavin tomorrow, at least this time she'd know who he was and what he wrote. It wasn't stalking, not really, but more... research. As an author, she knew it was perfectly acceptable to browse one's sites. They were out in the open about who they were. They had to be. The world often wanted to know the person behind their favorite books and these days, it was that information and interaction that played such a huge role when it came to sales. Facebook, Twitter, Goodreads, blogs, and websites, authors had it all. Not only did they bleed their hearts onto the pages of the books they wrote, but within the interaction they shared with their fans. Connecting with one person led to connecting with more, and each reader that knew an author's name was a potential sale of a book.

From Gavin's website to his Twitter, to a Wikipedia page, Piper read it all. His age popped up on one of the sites. She glanced at it briefly, making a mental note, subtracting the numbers, but not being bothered at all by it. It was insignificant. She was attracted to him and wouldn't let a number be a deciding factor if she were to get the chance to talk to him again. In fact, the more she thought about Gavin, the more certain she was that she wanted to get to know him. There was something there that she had to discover. That tickle in her tummy, that pitch of energy that drew her to him, almost summoning.

Inside her, coming out of nowhere, causing Piper to close the browser, shutting away the images of Gavin, a familiar whisper could be heard in the deepest corner of her mind. Barely audible but came with a surge of inspiration that could have only come from her muse.

Piper gasped, and opened up a blank document, the cursor blinking rapidly, waiting for her fingers to press the keys. She closed her eyes, inhaled a deep breath, the smell of Gavin materializing in the air around her as she let the whisper grow louder.

A character formed in her mind, the voice suddenly telling her what to type. Before Piper knew it, she banged out a few sentences, and then a few more. She felt exhilarated as more words leaped onto the page.

As the images of Gavin began to dissolve from her brain, the smell of his cologne no longer lingering in the air, and the warmth of his touch had completely turned cold, the whisper faded. Inspiration slipped through her, disappearing just as quickly as it had come until she was left with silence. A complete and utter feeling of despair.

Highlighting the words she'd typed, Piper then pounded her finger against the delete button. She turned the almost-filled page of black words back into a stark white screen of nothingness. A flash of anger gripped her heart as she slammed the lid of her laptop closed and shoved it off her lap.

Taking a pillow from behind her, Piper covered her face and screamed furiously into the feathers until her throat burned. Certain she was done, she pulled the pillow from her face, blinked back the fireworks that flashed in front of her eyes, and wiped at the tears that had formed.

What happened, she wondered? It was there, if for only a moment. Her muse had come back, but why couldn't it stay? That was the reason why she'd come to Northern Write Con in the first place. Hoping she could find it again, relish in the inspiration that poured from the other authors that surrounded her. Maybe she could have stolen a muse from someone else, welcoming it with open arms.

An idea, almost absurd, came forefront. Was that why her muse had left? Had she unknowingly neglected it, giving it a reason to pack its bags and move on? Perhaps finding another host, another soul, that would treat it better, listen to it when it spoke, telling the stories it wanted to be written?

Piper laughed out loud. It was impossible. It had to be. She hadn't turned her back on her muse, had she? She thought about the past, recreating the last year's events in her mind, playing the movie that was her life. There were so many changes that had taken place. A move, a crumbling relationship, and a job she had taken to pay her bills... Before that, she'd sat at her computer, struggling to adapt the latest ideas her muse had shared with her. She had fought back hard, unwilling to change her genre, despite the urgings of her muse.

Piper wrote strictly Young Adult. Sensual love stories, coming-of-age novels for every reader. Female characters that finally discovered who they were, and how to maneuver through adolescence. Piper kept them clean, free of the clutter that had begun to take over the market, where boundaries were often pushed. Sex, drugs and alcohol seemed to sell, and Piper's muse knew that, pushing her in that direction—an older target audience, where it would be able to unleash its innermost desires.

That's when things started to go wrong. Piper suddenly forced her characters into awkward situations, only to leave them hanging inside unfinished stories, because she was averse to change. She didn't want her characters to shed clothes, morals, and become just like every other book out there, even if she was absorbed with those kinds of novels herself.

The need in her own life was to spark the fire when it came to her sexual desires, desperate for something that would make her feel alive. Books did that. When she felt her own libido waning—which may have been the cause for her break up—the mention of a nipple, the stroke of a hardened cock, or the illicit moans of an orgasm awakened her. Filling her with that lust she had long since lost. It warmed her to the core. Yet, she refused to use that newfound love of erotica and channel it into her own writing.

More, perhaps, she couldn't. She didn't know how. Even as she read the books that caused a twitch between her legs, a swell of wetness that caressed her panties, she felt she could never find the right words. Piper worried her readers would see through the facade she'd have to create. Worse, call her out as an inexperienced shrew who didn't know how to tell a story filled with romance, strong characters, and sex that created orgasmic release through a collection of well-written prose.

But that had been what her muse wanted. An exploration of something entirely different, and new. Ideas that might break way for novels that would actually sell. Piper wouldn't give in. She wouldn't let the muse control her.

She pressed the palms of her hands against her eyes, pushing away the tears. It was her fault. Losing her muse had been by her own doing.

Although, that still didn't answer why it had come to her that night. Whispering in her ear just loud enough to create that sense of urgency, the unbearable need to write words onto the page. And why so swiftly it went away, taking with it the hint of the character it began to form in her mind.

Then, as if to answer the question she silently asked, the night's events tumbling back, she swore she understood. That innate urge to write had been fuelled by the presence of a stranger who suddenly came into her life.

It was the only difference. The connection of their skin, the flutter of butterflies in her stomach, and the yearning to be wrapped in his arms, to pick his brain and learn the knowledge he held there.

Gavin.

He was the one who stole her muse. He had to be. Or maybe, hadn't stolen it, but welcomed her muse into him with the acceptance of what it wanted to share. His bibliography was long, books coming out recently, and many more in the future. He seemed to have no trouble weaving words together to create remarkable, unforgettable stories. Piper even read somewhere, that many of his works of fiction contained the very erotic element her muse had tried to push her towards, yet she refused it.

So the question now begged, if Gavin had her muse, how was she to get it back?

* * *

The sheets were tangled tightly around Piper when she awoke with a start. Her head craned to see the clock, the flicker of numbers telling her she overslept. More than overslept, yet she felt exhausted. A restless night caused unwarranted dreams to take over. She felt damp with sweat, threads of short mahogany hair plastered to her face, her eyes barely willing to stay open. All she wanted to do was draw the curtains tight and remain in bed for the foreseeable future.

But she couldn't do that. She had a mission to carry out; one where she'd take back her muse, forcibly if she had to. Piper refused to leave Northern Write Con without it firmly reattached to her soul, and she was willing to do whatever it took to make that happen.

Spending the better part of the morning, Piper poured over the day's programming schedule. However, it seemed just as fate and her muse had brought her and Gavin together, now it was doing everything it could to tear them apart. Her schedule was nearly full with her own panels, that—annoyingly enough—seemed to be when Gavin had time off from his.

After making a few deep red circles in her program, Piper began to get ready for the day. She spent extra time on her hair, smoothing down the unruly and out of place strands. She swept on concealer, eye shadow and even lipstick—something she rarely did, relying more heavily on the tube of green chap-stick she carried with her everywhere. This wasn't just a regular day; she needed to pull out as many stops as she could.

Once her makeup was done, hair in place, Piper rummaged through her suitcase and scolded herself for the rush pack job she had done. Back then, she hadn't cared about what she brought, more concerned with comfort over style. What she really needed now was a low cut, skin-baring top, tight pants and some heels. Something that would make her the bombshell she often craved to be, but knew she never could. Her head shook at the thought, knowing that even if that kind of outfit had found its way into her suitcase, she'd never have the courage to wear it. Not in public. Not where people would see and be forced to look at the flaws she hated.

She wasn't fat, per se, but she'd packed on a few extra pounds she could stand to do without, making her less desirable to most of the men out there. Her skin wasn't clear, but rather held blemishes, rosy cheeks, and a few wrinkles creasing her forehead. The kind of flaws that no amount of makeup could ever really cover up.

Slipping on another pair of jean capri's, a graphic t-shirt with the barest of lace revealing a small amount of her back, and her sneakers, Piper chanted a mantra in her head. She needed to work up the courage to leave the hotel room. Even more as she walked the same path she was sure Gavin would take to and from his panels, desperate to see him again. She was nearly five minutes late to every one of hers, taking the long way around, but as the day drew to a close, she hadn't caught the slightest glimpse of him.

Piper's attention wasn't where it should have been; immersing herself in conversations about books, and writing, and how to create compelling scenery, realistic dialogue, or trying to gauge the next big trend. It was on her muse, and Gavin. She knew her panels had suffered from her inability to stay focused, but didn't care.

At the end of the day, when the conference was winding down, Piper was drained. She half-heartedly waved goodbye or hugged her fellow authors, bidding them farewell and safe travels. That sinking feeling in the pit of her stomach was back. She had searched the crowds that spilled out of the ballrooms, until she realized she'd missed out on her chance to see Gavin again, and get her muse back.

Sluggishly, she headed towards the elevator as the last of her friends left. Her hotel room, booked for one more night, was calling her name. The down-filled pillow, the soft blanket, and the idea of a dark room, begged for her. She'd go upstairs, shut herself away, and maybe drown her misery in the lonely bottle of beer still left in her fridge from the night before. In the morning she'd head home and begin to face the reality that she was never getting her muse back. She'd written the creativity right out of herself. From the world's perspective, she'd become that author who wrote two books, only to never write again.

Piper wasn't watching where she was going, and yelped in surprise when she collided with a hard body, nearly toppling over. Strong arms held her upright as she muttered a thanks, self-consciously smoothing down the hem of her shirt.

"You're still here," the voice spoke to her.

That familiar surge found its way into her body as she looked up through hooded eyes. Trying to remain calm, Piper replied, "You're still here," putting on a smile she hoped didn't give away her excitement.

"Yeah, I'm headed home in the morning," Gavin said, releasing his hold on her.

She stepped back, giving him a wide berth, not wanting to invade his personal space, no matter how much she wanted to cling to him. "Yeah, me too." She tucked hair behind her ear and toed the ground with her sneaker, suddenly nervous.

"Are you going to the dead dog?"

Her eyebrows furrowed as she forced her attention back towards him.

"The dead dog social, tonight?"

"Oh, um, I didn't know there was one." Elation eclipsed the nervousness she felt a moment ago. This was it, the chance she'd been waiting for.

"Yeah, sort of a wind-down kind of thing. I heard there might be drinks."

A drink she needed, if she was going to remain calm, collected and figure out how to get her muse away from him. A crackle of electricity charged the air between them and with it came the hum of her muse. "Sounds like fun. What time?"

The elevator doors opened with a chime. Gavin took a tentative step forward, turning back slightly. "Seven-thirty. You should come. It'll beat hanging around an empty hotel by yourself."

Piper looked around. The commotion of the last three days had disappeared in a flurry. She was having a hard time imagining the way it looked, even just hours ago, with hundreds of people taking up most square inches of space. "Thanks. I think I will."

With a nod, Gavin slipped through the doors of the elevator just as they began to close. He turned and gave her one last consuming look that melted her from the inside out.

She was definitely going to the social. The way her heart skittered in her chest made her realize she was still very much attracted to the man who held captive her muse, which further complicated things. Either way, she knew the night would end on a high note, she was sure of it.

When she pulled out her phone, the clock told her the night wouldn't be starting for a couple more hours. She'd have to find something to do in the meantime to calm the restless itch she felt.

When seven-thirty arrived, Piper took the elevator to the second floor. She'd been foolish, forgetting to ask where the social was happening. As the stepped off onto the second floor, she could hear conversations coming at her from all sides. It seemed there were still lots of people left over from the conference, ready for one last hooray, ending Northern Write Con for another year.

She chose a direction and headed towards the closest set of voices, poking her head through an open door. A few people sat, drinks in hand, in a circle of chairs. A girl strummed a guitar and a friendly face smiled, a hand waving at Piper. She returned it, but at the disappointment that came from not spotting Gavin sitting in the group, she moved on.

The next open door made way to a bunch of conference goers sitting around a large table, stacks of intricate and colorful cards laid out over the top. They were in deep conversation, playing a game that Piper vaguely remembered from high school, but again, there was no Gavin.

Another room yielded more conference stragglers, but none resembled the tall, masculine man she was in search of. As a wave of disappointment threatened to cloud Piper, bringing down her spirits, she realized there was one more room she hadn't yet explored. A little faster on her feet, she headed towards the weekend hospitality suite. A hold-all of everything a starving writer could need; bottles of water, coffee, cans of soda and snacks. Piper had found herself there a few times over the weekend, ducking her head in just long enough to grab a soda and a cookie from the tray of baked goods, or sneaking a few extra bottles of water to store in her hotel room fridge for later.

Piper rounded the corner, headed towards the last place Gavin could possibly be if he'd planned to attend the evening festivities. She heard the voice, calling out to her like a beacon. It took all her restraint not to run the last distance, instead casually entering the room, the busiest of them all.

The temperature definitely rose a few degrees as she stepped over the threshold, more than a dozen mingling bodies cramping the small space. And there, right by the door, leaning against the wall, was Gavin, a beer bottle in his hand, wearing that smile she hadn't realized she'd missed.

The trick now was figuring out what to do, now that Gavin was finally in her sights.

Piper slid down the wall and joined him where he stood. She stayed silent, trying to follow along with the conversation, until Gavin paused, noticing her presence.

"You came," he said, sounding almost excited to see her. His delicious hazel eyes brightened.

"Yeah, well, I didn't have much else to do, and I heard there'd be booze."

"Great, well, let's get you a drink."

From out of nowhere, a fresh beer was thrust towards Piper and she wasted no time taking a long pull from the neck of the bottle. Liquid courage. Either that or a really awful idea. Only time would tell.

Gavin seemed to be the center of conversations, being pulled in one direction or another, and keeping close to him proved difficult. She needed to stay close. Piper swore every time his hand innocently brushed against hers, she heard the titter of her muse whispering, reaching out, trying to reattach itself.

However, as the night dragged on, Piper was no closer to her end game. She'd yet to capture his attention entirely. Nor devise a plan to steal back her muse. She found herself wandering through the lobby, out the doors, and into the growing night for a cigarette just to calm her nerves. The beers she'd consumed were catching up to her, warmth running through her veins, the gentle buzz of the alcohol slowly gnawing away at her inhibitions; the time also ticking away like a bomb ready to explode.

She made her way back to the second floor, another round of courage fueling her steps, as she realized the cramped party at the hospitality suite had moved to a bigger conference room. Piper was able to find a chair open and luckily for her, it was right next to Gavin. Finally, the break she needed.

Conversation this time came effortlessly, the liquor buzz becoming useful. She was able to join in, and found herself talking to Gavin with little pressure. For a moment, she wasn't terrified. She felt safe, and her muse spoke louder to her than ever before the more intimate the conversation grew.

There were new faces, and Gavin was kind enough to introduce Piper, seeming to know just about everyone in the room.

After a few more beers, Piper had finally relaxed enough to let her true personality shine through, just as it seemed Gavin took to flirting with her. But then, she wasn't completely sure.

"We should have music," someone said. "Does anyone have any speakers?"

Piper joined the consensus, saying, "Music would be great."

Looking right at her, Gavin said, "I do, up in my room," with a suggestive tone.

"Would you go get it and bring it down here?" someone asked.

"Maybe later," Gavin replied, his eyes still focused on Piper.

A few minutes later they engaged in a conversation about music, the two laughing. Gavin's hand found Piper's knee and gave it a squeeze. The whisper of her muse yelled something Piper couldn't discern, but quieted down when his touch slipped away.

"Shit. My drink's empty," Piper said to no one in particular, but then Gavin was right there, a gentle hand back on her knee as he leaned in towards her.

"I think I might have some, up in my room." His warm breath tickled her neck, sending a shiver up her spine.

She laughed; that expression had become the running joke of the night. Piper could make a list a mile long of all the things Gavin had up in his room. It was everything from a pen, an ARC of his latest novel, candy, to the skeleton he often toted around with him as part of his author branding. All of which he tried to use as a way to entice her, spoken with an intimate tone, longing hazel eyes, and most definitely directed at her.

* * *

"I'm not leaving. Not unless Piper comes with me, up to my room," Gavin said to a conference goer sitting across from them. Someone must have been demanding an item from his hotel room. She had tuned out the most recent conversations. But that was a clear-cut invitation. And it exploded her core with intensity. It burned hot, and she almost fell out of her chair. Gavin was quick to push her back to center, his warm hand searing the exposed skin of her arm.

She turned slightly towards him, licking her lips, relishing in the heat that came from his tender touch.

"So, will you? Come up to my room?"

Piper flushed with excitement as she looked away.
He leaned closer. "Please."

Turning back towards him, she found herself at a loss for words. Her muse began to take over, the chatter inside her head growing so loud it was about all she could hear. She realized Gavin's hand was still resting on her arm. She looked down at it, the connection they shared, and searched his eyes to find they were filled with the same desire she was sure was being exuded from hers.

"I don't know if I'm drunk enough," she said innocently, thrusting her empty bottle towards him.

"Well, I said it before, I've got more beer, up in my room."

Piper licked her lips again as her muse continued to rage on inside her. She swore she began to feel it crawling from Gavin's hand, up her arm, spreading over her. It tried to reconnect with her, stitching itself to her veins, figuring out how to gain access to her soul. Piper was sure it would only take a few more minutes, but then Gavin pulled his hand from her, severing the bond between them.

The muse protested, ringing in her ears, trying to stay entwined with the host it now desperately wanted to be a part of. All too soon the loud yelling became less audible until it was a low murmur, and then, gone again.

Though Piper wasn't sure it was a good idea to go to Gavin's room just yet, she did manage to say, "Maybe, you should go get it." She batted her eyelashes.

He stood from his chair. "I'll be back," he tossed over his shoulder and made his way towards the door in long calculated strides. The exit so hasty, it left Piper reeling.

Now, not only was the mumble of her muse gone, but so was Gavin, and Piper unexpectedly regretted sending him away. She counted to ten in her head, stood from her chair and said, "I'll be back, just going outside for a smoke," to no one, in particular.

Piper headed for the elevator, reaching it in time to see the doors slip closed, Gavin inside. She pushed the button and impatiently waited for the other elevator. She could follow him up to the 14th floor, she was sure of it. When the doors finally opened, Piper stepped inside, her heart racing.

She stuck in her key card, pressed the button that would take her to Gavin, only it wouldn't stay lit. Cursing aloud, she tried again. Key card in slot. Press 14. The light still wouldn't stay on. The elevator wouldn't move. Finally, she realized the catastrophic error she'd made. Her room was on the 9th floor, which meant that was as high up in the elevator as she could go.

Piper punched the wall, slammed her thumb over the button that would take her to the lobby and tried to ignore her devastation.

She wandered through the empty hotel, and the farther she got from the party, and Gavin, the sicker she felt. The loss of connection pulled her muse away again, just as she wondered, was it really that simple? Yet a cruel joke? The irony of the situation caused her to laugh out loud.

Suddenly, she knew how to get her muse back.

Maybe she'd known all along and didn't take it for what it was. She'd have to do something unimaginable. Release inhibitions she kept locked away tight, and for once, simply indulge in what she wanted most but never allowed herself to have.

A night of unadulterated bliss. No strings attached. She wanted to be taken the way the women in novels were, but could never bring herself to write about. In part, because she'd never experienced something so spontaneous and out of character. That's why she'd turned down her muse's relentless suggestions to switch genres. How could she write about something she knew nothing about?

Her experimentations, when it came to anything outside the norm, weren't winning her any awards in the risqué department. Hell, she'd never done it on anything that wasn't a bed. Maybe this was just the push needed to step outside her comfort zone. Way outside it. Gavin was apparently taken by her, being flirtatious and asking—in more ways than one—if she'd accompany him up to his room. And she, undoubtedly, was attracted to him; the muscles in her stomach tightened merely at the thought. New warmth spread over her cheeks at the mere possibility of his hands exploring her body, his lips kissing the gentle contours of her skin.

Yes, she was more than a little attracted to him, it turned out. Just the idea of his body pressed against hers sent a surge of desire through her, awakening even the most sensitive parts of herself.

She tossed her half-smoked cigarette away and turned towards the lobby. Using the glass of the entrance as her mirror, Piper adjusted her T-shirt, fluffed up her hair and applied a little more lipstick. Inhaling a deep breath, she closed her eyes, focusing on the mission of reclaiming her muse. Yet, as confident as she felt, she was still unsure if she'd be able to follow through in the end. She wanted it. Badly. But timid might as well have been Piper's middle name. That was a characteristic of herself she would never be able to change. She didn't think she could be as forward and direct, telling him what she truly wanted, as he seemed to be able with her. She had to be willing to at least try.

Of course, she also knew that nothing ever really came with no strings attached. A night like this would change them both. One of them was probably going to get hurt in the process. Mostly likely Piper.

* * *

As Piper took one more deep calming breath, she felt a current prickle the back of her neck, raising the hairs on her arms. That odd sensation of being watched, eyes boring into the back of her head. Piper swallowed. Gradually, she lifted her eyes, catching sight of another reflection in the glass. Just a second ago, she'd been alone, and yet, Gavin now stood behind her. He held a beer in one hand and two paper cups in the other.

"I thought I'd come down and find you." His eyes searched hers for a reaction.

She sucked in another breath, slowly turning around as her heart skittered in her chest. "I'm glad you did," she spoke honestly, smiling up at him, ignoring the miniscule tug of her conscience that was questioning how he'd managed to sneak up on her. She swore her eyes had only been closed for a moment, not to mention, having a clear view of the lobby made it even more peculiar.

"Are you ready to head back inside?"

Piper wasn't sure if it was the cool summer breeze or the closeness of Gavin, but a shiver ran up her spine. She nodded in answer, taking a step towards him. Gavin turned on his heels and together they walked through the lobby doors and towards the elevator. He juggled the beer in one hand and slipped his card into the slot. His fingers hovered over the button that would take them to the second floor, but Piper knew, this might be the last chance she'd ever have with him. Alone. She gently pushed his hand away and quickly pressed the button that would take them to his floor, and from there, to his hotel room.

"Are you sure?" He cleared his throat, sounding surprised, caught off guard by their sudden change in destination.

"I am. Besides, I hear the view from your floor is much better than from mine."

He laughed easily. "Well, I am up just that bit higher, which helps."

As the elevator counted up the floors, Piper grew surer of herself. He'd taken a step closer to her, arms brushed together again, and her muse was right there with them.

The door to Gavin's hotel room clicked closed behind Piper. The room, similar to hers, was filled with a king size bed, a small table, and two chairs. On the wall opposite the bed, a TV flickered on mute. She took a step farther in, as Gavin set down the beer and shrugged off his jacket. He laid it gently on the back of a chair. Tonight he was wearing brown slacks, a black button up shirt and the discarded jacket, a charcoal gray. He undid the buttons on his sleeves and rolled them up one at a time, as he asked, "Would you like a drink?"

"Sure. I mean, yes, please. I'd love one," Piper responded, as she took another step into the room but hesitated, suddenly unsure of where she should be. Would sitting on the bed seem too eager and suggestive? Or would the chair across from it make their encounter feel too casual? The argument with herself didn't last long. She settled on standing and watched as Gavin carefully popped the top off the beer and poured two paper cups full.

He closed the distance and offered her the drink. Eagerly, she took one of the cups and downed the contents in two large mouthfuls. A little more liquid courage, at that point, could only help matters. She'd come this far, and if she left now, she'd only be a tease.

"Can I get you more?" He motioned to the empty cup in her hand, eyeing her curiously.

She hated that his features gave nothing away. Gavin seemed so calm, collected, whereas she was still trying to suppress any lingering doubts. "Sure," she replied, handing it back over to him. He filled it again and moved towards her, this time stopping even closer, toe to toe, towering over her. "Thanks." She downed the alcohol just as quickly as she had the first time.

"Easy there," he said, taking the cup and setting it on the TV stand. He swallowed. "Are you nervous?"

"No. I mean, yes. Maybe, a little." She shook her head and let out an exasperated sigh.

"Look, I wanted you up here. That was pretty obvious. But I don't want to do anything you're not comfortable with." His tone was soft as he reached forward, gently brushing the side of her cheek with his fingers.

Biting her lip, it took Piper a second to reply. "I'm comfortable," she said, surprising herself, as she realized she wasn't lying. At all. She felt relaxed and safe. And though she'd only just met him, she could tell Gavin was a gentleman. He wanted what she wanted, but he wouldn't force her to do anything she wasn't ready to do.

Gavin set his untouched drink down next to hers and then stepped forward, dissolving the last bit of distance between them. He opened his arms and pulled her into him, a tight embrace. This time, however, he let his hands wander; at first, smoothing down her back gently. His touch was barely there, but then pressing harder as his hands swept back up. He paused at her shoulders, giving them a reassuring squeeze, before letting them drift again. By the time Gavin pulled away slightly, her face was cradled in his hands.

Their separation lasts only a few beats of Piper's heart until he was leaning back into her. Inching closer and closer. She swallowed, licking her lips to wet them, eyes instinctively fluttering closed; anticipation taking over, waiting for his lips to fall upon hers.

Only, they didn't. Not right away. Instead, Gavin's warm breath caressed her ear one more time as he whispered, "You're sure. This is what you want?" Eager to gain her approval, he patiently waited for her response by resting his chin on her shoulder.

"Yes. I'm sure. I-I want this."

In answer, Gavin shifted his stance and placed his lips delicately against hers. She tuned out the sound of her Muse wailing in the background as she wrapped her arms around him, drawing Gavin in even closer. It forced their touch to deepen, the kiss now carrying a sense of urgency.

A burst of sensation spread over every inch of Piper, signaling each nerve ending, sparking them with electricity. She felt her muse then, trying to claw free, pushing itself towards her. It craved the connection, just as much as she did, but for different reasons. It desperately wanted to escape and settle back into her soul, and yet, Piper frantically wanted to push herself closer to Gavin.

He dropped his hands from her face and trailed them down her neck, over the front of her shirt, gently cupping both her breasts. Even with the fabric of the shirt and bra between them, she let out a moan. He broke the kiss, moved his hands from her and settled them on her hips. With little fight from her, he spun her around, pressing her into his chest.

She could feel his enthusiasm protruding, pushing against her, as Gavin held her close. He swept her hair to the side, then made a line of soft, wet kisses from just beneath her ear, down her neck. He tugged at her shirt, revealing her shoulder, where he continued to place his lips on every inch of exposed skin. Piper let out another moan as his hand dipped beneath the fabric, pushing aside her lacy bra, and cupped her breast again. She marveled at the feel of his strong hand against her as fingers teased and tugged at her nipple.

Piper grew wet with pleasure as she gained the bravery needed to return some of the attention he was giving her. Her hand slid between them, skimming over the belt of his pants, to where his arousal was even more evident than before. She took as much of him into her palm as she could. Slowly she stroked her hand over his length as he continued to tease her nipple.

Gavin's touch began to further explore the contours of Piper's body. Down her hip, across her thigh, and then lightly back up until his hand settled between her legs, at the core of her warmth. Piper let out an involuntary shudder, eager for him to continue discovering her most delicate areas.

Her hips rolled again, bucking against Gavin's steady hand. Finally, taking that as a go ahead, he wasted no time pulling the button on her jeans free. Piper gasped as he plunged his hand down the front. His deft actions were calculated, sliding his palm down her front, underneath her panties until his fingers found the wetness between the folds of her skin. Slowly, he moved his fingers over her, circling her.

As the buildup of pressure intensified, Piper's knees began to wobble. She wanted more. Wanted his fingers inside her, ready to know what it would feel like, but Gavin had other plans. He pulled his hands back, only to fist the hem of her shirt in his palms.

His minty, warm breath tickled her neck again as he asked, "May I?" giving the fabric a tug, just as Piper nodded against his chest.

His hands then slid up the length of her torso, pushing Piper's arms over her head, taking the shirt up with the movement. She gave the material, now discarded on the floor, a cursory glance as Gavin's soft touch glided over her again, bringing her arms back down to her sides. With skillful fingers Gavin was able to release the clasp of her bra; freeing her breasts and sliding the straps free. That too, landed somewhere on the floor as Piper's breath caught in her throat, her heart suddenly colliding violently in her ribcage, causing her to stiffen.

Gavin sensed her change in demeanor instantly. "It's okay," he said. "If you're feeling too exposed, we can stop." He circled his arms around Piper, covering her breasts, holding her tightly to him.

Piper silently cursed. "No. I-I don't want to stop," she said, but even to her it sounded nervous, forced. She pinched her eyes shut, expecting Gavin to pull away, ending the evening. Instead, however, he simply held her. She hated herself at that moment, feeling insecure and constrained. That silly girl who wore her inexperience and uncertainty so obviously. But she knew she wanted Gavin more than anything, and though she desperately wanted her muse back, it took second place to needing him to consume her.

"It's just been awhile," she said honestly, allowing the comfort Gavin gave her to aid in gaining control of her raging heart and calming herself down.

This time when Gavin spoke, his tone held his own nervousness as he said, with a slightly awkward chuckle, "If we're being honest, it's been quite a long while for me, too."

The response didn't make sense to Piper. She tilted her chin up and searched his eyes. The hazel smoldered, a flash of sadness consuming them. She wanted to ask what he meant by that. It seemed impossible for someone as handsome and commanding as he to not have had anyone share his bed on a frequent basis. Piper truly believed Gavin could have any woman he wanted. She still wondered, if not for the fact that he held her muse, why he'd chosen her. Out of the hordes of woman that must have batted their eyes at him, or pouted their lips, over the course of the weekend, his options should have been endless.

"I want this," Piper said after a second, pushing the remaining self-doubt aside. It didn't matter why he'd chosen her. What mattered was that she was there with him and that still, with his arms secured around her, she could hear the murmur of her muse calling out. She inhaled a breath and pulled Gavin's hands free.

Biting her lip as she turned to face him, Piper resisted the urge to cover herself, instead concentrating on the intense gaze he presented to her, and the lopsided grin that yanked away the tension in the air. It gave her the confidence she needed.

She went to tug her pants down, but Gavin was quick to stop her as he said, "Wait. Let me..." He trailed off as he quickly undid the buttons on his shirt, pulling the fabric down his arms, tossing it carelessly aside. "Just so you don't feel like the only one who is exposed." Gavin drew his belt open, yanked on the button of his pants, and slid down the fly. Slowly, he drew them down, taking his boxers along too, until he was standing in front of her more exposed to the world than she was.

The only thing Piper could concentrate on was his erection. A dominant sight, it caused a twitch of desire between her legs. But she was thankful for his gesture of exposing himself first. When she went to the waist of her jeans, Gavin took two quick steps towards her, placing his hands over hers. He grinned brightly at her as he helped her push down the last of her clothing.

Piper swallowed as Gavin took her hand in his. He pulled her towards the bed. This was it, she thought as she climbed over the plush bedspread, lying down on her back. Gavin followed her lead until he was hovering over her.

"You're still sure?" he asked again, needing to gain her permission before taking things to the next level.

With a breathless, barely audible sigh that might have sounded something like a yes from Piper, Gavin lowered himself against her. His lips found hers as he slowly pressed himself against her entrance.

Gently, he eased into her, barely the tip, before sliding back. As he took her bottom lip in his mouth, giving it the barest bite with his teeth, he slid himself towards her again. This time, he gave her more as her tight core clenched around his firmness. She took in each glorious inch, quivering beneath him, emitting the most delicious sounds through parted lips.

Her hands confidently reached around, grabbing his backside, forcing him to thrust deeper. Piper began to feel awakened with a surge of desire. He made calculated movements, pausing briefly every so often to lean towards her, pulling one of her nipples into his mouth, before resuming his pace. Gavin kissed her urgently as their two bodies melded together.

The air around them grew humid from the heat between them. Sweat began to form on Gavin's brow; a sheen covering Piper as she wrapped her legs tightly around his torso. She provoked him to shift his angle of penetration. Her core flared as the friction built, his body sliding against hers as though they were two perfectly shaped pieces of a puzzle. All the while, her muse grew vehement as she felt it seep from him, the connection that broadened, drawing them closer to release.

This is what the muse wanted. She knew it. And as the buildup became more insistent, so did Piper's assurance that she was doing the right thing. Gavin had a dominance over her, but then she was quick to take it from him, hoping to find that ultimate release she hadn't realized how much she needed. That final moment she was sure would allow her muse to stitch itself back into her soul.

She nudged him with a smile and said, "I think it's my turn to do some of the work." In a fluid motion that caused Piper to yelp with surprise, Gavin managed to pull her over, rolling until he was on the bottom. Suddenly, she was straddling him. He panted, chest heaving as he fought for a breath.

Gavin smirked up at her, taking in the sight of the smile that tugged at her heart, filling it with a hint of sadness. She loved the way he focused on her, but knew it was something that would never last.

Slowly, Piper began to move her hips, sliding up and down the length of Gavin's engorged erection, amazed at how he was able to fit entirely inside of her. He matched her movements as she worked her hips, up and down, and swirling them in a circle. The mounting pressure, the screams of her muse spurred her on as she leaned forward, digging her fingers into the hard wood of the headboard.

She gasped aloud, begging for more of Gavin's touches, desperate to have his searing hands on whatever part of her they could reach as she became feverish with determination. It didn't take long, Gavin's hands cupping her breasts, before she felt his muscles strain beneath her. With a grunt that tickled her insides, Gavin dropped his hands to her backside, squeezing her tightly as he pushed her harder and deeper than she ever thought possible. He came with a force that threatened to pull Piper along with him.

She kept her pace, desperate to continue, as he began to languish. Gavin had all but stopped seconds before she found her own release. As she called out, saying his name, for the briefest of moments she forgot her muse entirely. Her attention concentrated more on the hunger that continued to flare between them.

However, she did, if only for a second, smile proudly. She'd been taken, adorned with kisses, sensual touches, and filled with an orgasm like no other.

* * *

It was early morning by the time Piper slipped from Gavin's grasp, pushing herself off the bed. She gathered her clothes silently. The ache between her legs never seemed fully satiated. The more she was touched, teased, and licked, the more she craved him.

Gavin wordlessly pulled on his pants and shrugged his shirt over his shoulders as she began to get dressed.

Once she was ready to leave, Gavin took another business card from his pocket, holding it between them. Hesitantly, she took it, clutching it in her hand as the silence grew deafening.

Before Piper could protest, Gavin's strong arms wrapped tightly around her body. She breathed him in one last time, inhaling his scent of masculine aftershave mixed with the sweet stench of a one night stand.

He spoke softly, but his words were too casual, the night's events already dissipating from his mind. "Seriously. Shoot me an email. I want to hear all about your books."

Piper nodded against Gavin's chest, shirt open, fabric draped over toned muscles. "I will." She stepped out of his embrace, turning towards the door of the hotel room.

It was a lie.

She prayed she'd be able to reach for the door knob and disappear into the hallway without him seeing right through her. She didn't dare turn back, not allowing herself to give him one last fleeting gaze. That would only make things harder. Unbearable.

The door clicked closed, the sound resonating through the empty hallway. The blur of tears formed at the corners of her eyes as she found the elevator and feverishly pushed the down button.

She wished she could close her eyes, click her heels and be somewhere else.

Inside her own hotel room, she released her clutched hand, sending the business card into the trash. She had never planned on using it. Not really. She'd only gone to the conference to find her muse. It came from an unexpected place, tucked inside the body of a stranger she'd never see again.

Piper had managed to break it free. With an orgasm that shuddered through her as the last of her inhibitions drifted away, her muse had entangled itself with her again. It warmed her insides, sending a million story ideas to her brain, wrapping around her heart, and begged to be pushed out her fingertips as they pounded away at a keyboard.

Still reeling from the unimaginable night with Gavin, and thankful to have her muse back, she opened the lid to her laptop. The cursor blinked against the stark white and empty page. But that wouldn't be the case much longer.

As the first letters flowed through her—forming words, sentences, paragraphs, and finally, pages—Piper had never felt more alive. Her muse, now safely returned, was like the blood that pumped through her veins, the air she desperately needed to fill her lungs... It's what gave life to her. To her stories. Without it, she was nothing more than a person. A regular one, at that. It gave her the right to call herself an author. And it gave her the vision to create her next adventure, even if it was in a genre, for an age group, laced with innuendos, all too new to her.

Yet, as her fingers pressed excitedly on the keyboard, she wished getting her muse back hadn't meant she'd have to leave a piece of her heart behind.

Bonus Features

INSPIRATION CAN come from anywhere. Music is often used as a source for my inspiration, and I'm all too happy to share a bit of the playlist I used when creating these short stories.

In no particular order:

A Drop in the Ocean by Ron Pope
Hallelujah by Jeff Buckley
Let Her Go by Passenger
Fast Car by Tracy Chapman
Cryin' by Aerosmith
Ain't No Reason by Brett Dennen
Little Talks by Of Monsters and Men
The Freshman by The Verve Pipe
Wrap Your Arms Around Me by Gareth Dunlop
In This River by The Black Label Society
A Song for Someone by U2
Stay with Me by Sam Smith
Life Will Go On by Chris Isaak
If I Ever Leave this World by Flogging Molly

Dancing in the Moonlight by Toploader
Every Time We Touch by Groot
Kiss the Rain by Billie Myers
I Shall Believe by Sheryl Crow
Someone Like You by Adele
You and Me by Lifehouse

Acknowledgements

PERSONALLY, WHENEVER I get my hands on a new book, before I read the opening line and get sucked into the story itself, I read the acknowledgments. I'll skip right to the end, if I have to, just to do it. There's just something so interesting, and heartwarming, when it comes to reading about all the different people that we, as authors, have to thank. Those people that made a difference and helped us get to where we are today. It's a constant reminder, when often times, writing can be such a solitary sport, that we are never truly alone.

Because I didn't know where these stories would go, or if I'd ever do anything with them, I kept much of its creation under wraps. But had they known about it, I know my family and friends would have encouraged me, and supported me. Having people in my life that allow me the time to write is what truly deserves thanks.

When I was scrambling for Beta Readers, having no idea if these stories were any good, I really had to dig deep and put myself out there. I was scared. These stories were like nothing I'd ever written before. I owe so much to Mark Leslie, Steven Whibley, Chad Ganske, and Kathy Knull. I think a lot can be said about the fact that I was able to both entertain, hold the attention, and spark some reaction, from both my female and male readers. The ultimate compliment.

Erin Forbes. Venti Caramel Macchiatos and perusing the bookstore shelves is one of the best ways to relax, and sort through the tough stuff. I love that you get just as excited about my story ideas as I do, and are willing to talk about them endlessly. And you never lost your faith in me as a writer, even when I was sure I'd never write again.

Mark Leslie Lefebvre. Where do I even start? Words won't ever fully express how truly indebted I am to you for all that you have done. We're a million miles apart, but you're always there when I need you. A Padawan couldn't have asked for a better mentor. I'm not sure how I got so lucky. But meeting you has truly been an unforgettable experience :p

A huge thank you goes out to When Words Collide, Calgary, Alberta. It has brought me some remarkable friends and experiences, as it does every year, but I'm not sure how we can top the epicness that was the Fort O' Tablecloths in the lobby of 2014. I took **plenty** of liberties, but the start of this collection stemmed from that night. A perfect fit for a struggling author, desperate to find their muse. In no particular order, thank you; Tim R., Suzy V., Nola S., Aviva H., Adrienne K., Mark L., David F., Randy M., and about a million other people I wish I had space to name, but sadly, don't.

I suck at editing. Okay, there, I admitted it. Glad that's off my chest. I couldn't have gotten this collection of short stories in tip-top shape without the help of Jacquelyn Fox from Happy Endings Editing.

Have you taken a look at the cover? Okay, sure you have, but maybe check it out again, I'll wait. Isn't it gorgeous?! I am in LOVE with this cover. And I have to thank djole8 from 99Designs for going above and beyond!

And lastly, but certainly most importantly... Thank you to the readers. Everyone who curls up with my stories is deserving of a million warm fuzzies!

ABOUT THE AUTHOR

Madison Avery doesn't kiss and tell. Except when it comes to writing. She lives in Red Deer, Alberta, where she spends way too much time reading, writing and avoiding house work.

Capturing the Muse is her first foray into the world of erotica, but where she feels right at home.

You can find Madison, and her counterpart, Yong Adult Novelist, Avery Olive, on many social media sites like Facebook, Twitter (@AveryOlive), Tumblr, Goodreads and on her website, http://www.averyolive.blogspot.com

Made in the USA
Charleston, SC
06 August 2015